A CORPSE IN CAMERA

'Blood Bath at TV Studios — Film Star Decapitated.' Thus the evening newpapers describe a murder in which private eye Adam Flute has become hopelessly entangled. Originally hired by a worried wife to watch her husband, Flute only just manages to convince the police that he has nothing to do with the corpse he meets face to face. Two nymphettes, a middle-aged actress, an eccentric producer and two film stars make his enquiries exciting and glamorous — and fraught with danger.

Books by Drew Launay
in the Linford Mystery Library:

THE NEW SHINING WHITE MURDER
SHE MODELLED HER COFFIN
DEATH AND STILL LIFE

DREW LAUNAY

A CORPSE
IN CAMERA

Complete and Unabridged

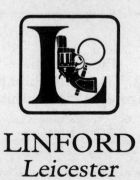

LINFORD
Leicester

First published in Great Britain in 1963
under the name of
'Droo Launay'

First Linford Edition
published 2001

British Library CIP Data

Launay, Droo, *1930* –
A corpse in camera.—Large print ed.—
Linford mystery library
1. Detective and mystery stories
2. Large type books
I. Title
823.9'14 [F]

ISBN 0–7089–4593–7

Published by
F. A. Thorpe (Publishing)
Anstey, Leicestershire

Set by Words & Graphics Ltd.
Anstey, Leicestershire
Printed and bound in Great Britain by
T. J. International Ltd., Padstow, Cornwall

This book is printed on acid-free paper

1

He was a tall man, six feet tall with a head of thick black hair, bright blue eyes and a dark suntanned skin. He was ruggedly handsome, his name was Justin Joyce and he was on the point of hurling himself from the parapet of a new apartment building to plunge a hundred and twenty feet to his death.

A large crowd watched him from below uncomfortably aware of the hard tarmac beneath them which his fourteen and a half stone body would hit like a soggy blood-soaked sponge. Eyes strained to catch his every movement as he edged himself a little nearer to the sharp corner of the high block.

He looked down, then quickly away, a gasp escaped from a thousand quivering lips as suddenly his twitching body jackknifed clear of the building to plummet to the ground in less than a second.

Women screamed, the crowd surged forward, an alarm bell rang and a siren wailed. It was all over. After three hours of waiting it was over and everyone would now be able to go home — after collecting their money.

As the extras moved away towards a side street, I made my way towards the block of flats that had served as main prop to the suicide scene.

An assistant director shouted at everyone through a megaphone and the sound unit retracted their microphones along the fishing-rod like booms. Near the all important cameras a dozen technicians told each other how lousy the morning had been and in the middle of it all, surrounded by the firemen who had held the safety mat, the stunt man took off his black wig and smiled at the real Justin Joyce who looked nothing like him.

'Great Joe!' an American voice drawled behind me. 'Glad it's over?'

'Bit scared the wind might cause a drift.'

Joe grinned, but not too widely, he had three scars across his face which told the ugly story of less successful jumps.

I turned around a little and took a good long look at the star of the picture. I was new to filming and had been taken in by the double's resemblance at a distance. Justin Joyce looked seedier than the last time I had seen him on the screen. His hair was getting grey at the temples and maybe a little too thin for a man of thirty-five. The thick locks of black hair that I had seen an Italian actress take so much pleasure running her fingers through seemed a bit too brittle to be natural, but he still had that amused cruel smile and those intense eyes.

The American director argued for a few minutes with one of the technicians before admitting that he was satisfied, turned to Joyce to tell him he could buzz off home, then gulped down half a pint of anti-ulcer milk which his secretary handed him. His name was Oscar Lovaks and he was the man I was being paid to watch.

★   ★   ★

Six days before I had been idling away my time kidding myself I could do the *Telegraph* crossword puzzle on the chilly windswept balcony of my flat overlooking the Bayswater Road. Down in the hallway of the block a discreet brass plate bore the legend: ADAM FLUTE. PRIVATE INVESTIGATOR. 6TH FLOOR.

This, even coupled with a regular advertisement in the higher strata magazines didn't bring me any clients. I had been contemplating taking up car salesmanship, or something equally difficult, when the doorbell had rung and an archangel had walked in.

She was getting on, as far as archangels go, hitting forty anyway, but she didn't remind me of my mother.

'Mr. Flute?' she had asked in a deep gossamer voice. 'My name is Zeelah Danton, and I was wondering whether you could help me.'

She was wearing an inexpensive Balmain two-piece with shoes to match the handbag which matched the suit. On three of her suntanned fingers she wore four rings with a gross of diamond carats attached.

4

'You're younger than I expected,' she said to me as I looked into her deep brown eyes. It wasn't often one got clients this attractive, her hair was made up of autumn tints and smelt of lethal sandalwood.

'Maybe you were expecting to see my uncle,' I said. 'He used to run the business but retired last year.' I gave her one of my charming smiles, usually reserved for the teenage market, and it worked like a dream.

'Do you follow people?' she asked, a little nervously perhaps, not sure what the title, Private Investigator, implied.

'All the time,' I said. 'Who did you want me to follow?'

'A man.'

'It makes a change.'

She smiled and settled more comfortably in the uncomfortable chair reserved for clients. I was sitting behind my half-acre leather-topped desk in front of the window with the light coming in from behind me and hitting her fair and square between the eyes.

'Can I have a few more details?' I

asked. I offered her a cigarette which she accepted, then I had to stand up to light it for her, the effort alone was worth the five-guinea consulting fee I had every intention of charging her.

'I'm an actress,' she started, smiling modestly to hide her pride, and blowing out a thin wisp of smoke. 'I was married to a man called Oscar Lovaks.'

I noted the name down on a note pad I had for that very purpose.

'I was also married to Justin Joyce.' She paused, not for effect, but to see how I would react.

'Justin Joyce,' she continued, 'is now a famous film star, but he wasn't when I first married him.'

I didn't say anything but noted down the name 'Justin Joyce, famous film star, remember — buy dozen eggs and two cans of beer'. The act was impressive.

'Justin divorced me three years ago and recently married Noelle Knowles.'

I nodded. I had heard of the wedding. It had filled the front pages of all the lousier newspapers for two days because Miss Knowles had arrived two hours late for the ceremony, during which time Mr. Joyce had held a champagne party in the vestry, which had necessitated finding a new priest for the service when the bride had finally turned up.

'Who do you want me to follow?' I asked, already imagining myself in Hollywood and getting into some D.A's hair.

'My first husband, Oscar Lovaks.'

'Why?'

'I received an anonymous letter telling me that he was having an affair with Noelle Knowles — I'd like to know if it's true.'

'Why?' One day I hoped to get the International Interviewers Award.

'That's my business — I'd just like to know if the rumour's true.'

Actresses don't get onto the stage without a certain amount of temperament. It was the first time she had shown she had any.

'Any idea where either of them might be?'

'Oscar is making a film starring Justin, but I've no idea where it's being made. They're probably on location somewhere and presumably Noelle is with Justin, or Oscar!'

I swivelled my swivel chair, looked up at the sky through the window and tried to estimate how much I could sting her for. She obviously guessed what I was up to.

'What do you charge?'

'You can either hire me by the day or settle for a fixed sum, paying half in advance and half on completion of the investigation. Expenses are extra in both cases.'

'Which would you advise?'

'If you buy me by the day I don't work for anyone else, just you. It's quicker, may only take a day or two instead of a fortnight.'

She settled for the day tariff and I settled back in my chair. She was either the type who liked owning her men or she was in a hurry. But who was I to care, I'd soon be able to eat again.

* * *

The Federation of British Film Industries traced Oscar Lovaks for me after three telephone calls. He was working in the South of France on location near Cannes shooting his new film *Lonely Are the Damned*. They didn't know where Noelle Knowles was, but suggested I should try her agent.

The agency were very kind and told me that Miss Knowles was on holiday in Cannes, they also told me that she had only made one film *Opus 23* in which she had played the part of a mad composer's neurotic sister. The casting, they hinted, had been spot on. Miss Knowles was a bit dippy — though absolutely charming. I thanked them, thought about the fifteen per cent they were taking off her income and was thankful that I wasn't involved in the business.

Somehow I failed to get a plane reservation for Nice till the following morning, which added a good twelve hours on to Miss Danton's expense sheet, but finally I took off from London Airport about eight, to arrive in the blazing sun of the Cote d'Azure in time for breakfast. No one met me, no one knew I was coming — I was as lonely as the damned.

It took me three hours to locate Lovaks film unit, half-an-hour to hire a car, and half-an-hour to get from my hotel to the new estate up in the hills where the giant block of flats was being used for the film.

* ⋆ *

After watching the stunt man jump, all I had to do was watch Lovaks and he would lead me to his private life without even knowing that someone was interested.

As I edged my way towards the huddle of camera men I found myself facing Justin Joyce searching his pockets for a match. I offered him the end of my cigarette and waited till his was lit before making the most of the encounter. 'Your wife with you, Mr. Joyce?' I asked.

He gave me a pained look, his eyes hated my tie, his long fingers squeezed his cigarette.

'Joke?'

The puzzled expression on my face as I watched him walk on, rang a little sympathy from the stunt man, Joe, who was following him.

'That was a whopper, Mac, wasn't it?' he said studying me with suspicion.

'Why? What's happened?'

'He found his wife dead this morning, with a hundred weight of sleeping tablets inside her guts.'

2

I wasn't invited but I went all the same. The lounge was crowded with reporters, the bars were full of them and so was the lift to the fourth floor where Noelle Knowles had her suite.

The French police weren't too interested in the case and were waiting for an English official to come. They realized the potential publicity this might mean for the hotel, which catered for film stars, and they didn't frighten away the journalists. As it was easier for me to pretend I was one of them, I slouched around and talked incessantly about people I didn't know making sure no one asked me who I represented.

The receptionist, when she was through with an American lad who was more fond of her wrist than his job, told me which room Oscar Lovaks had booked for himself. It was right next to the suite which Noelle Knowles had and there didn't seem to be any secret about the affair. Even Justin Joyce, when he came through the swing doors looking tired, just shrugged his shoulders to the Press when they asked him how he felt about his wife committing suicide, and did he know she had done so in his producer's bedroom?

My problem wasn't in the hotel any more, it wasn't even to confirm the affair between Lovaks and Knowles. My problem was to work out why Zeelah Danton had bothered to hire me to find out what she could have learnt simply by lifting up a telephone and dialling anyone in the film biz, or even in Fleet Street.

Realizing that this was a job I wouldn't make much on I decided to ring up my client and at least get the news of Noelle's death to her before she read it in the morning papers. I waited about an hour for a telephone, it was in the bar and I saw no reason why I should move, besides the conversations one could overhear were interesting. One reporter right next to me was telling his friend that Laminated Wools Ltd. had invested a vast sum in the Lovaks film because the chairman of the company was a woman who liked Justin Joyce. When I finally got the telephone I asked for Zeelah Danton's number.

'This is Adam Flute, Miss Danton. I've located the persons you were enquiring about, they're in Cannes.'

'Together?'

'They were, they separated this morning.'

'Oh. Who left who?'

'The lady left the gentleman.'

'Do you know where she went? Are they likely to meet again . . . secretly?'

'I doubt it. She's dead.'

'Dead? Noelle dead? I don't believe it!' From the tone of her voice it was obvious she didn't, she was laughing.

'Are you sure?'

'As sure as the hundred and fifty press men that are here.'

'Oh, I don't think much of that Mr. Flute, I expected better results from you.'

I didn't quite understand her, felt insulted, and said so.

'Unless you've actually seen Miss Knowles dead, I wouldn't believe it. It's probably a publicity stunt.'

I took a sip of my fine a l'eau and thought about it for a moment. Lovaks hadn't seemed very concerned on the location set and Joyce had just seemed bored.

'Is that the sort of stunt she goes in for?' I asked.

'No, not her, but Oscar would. I heard he was a bit short of funds for the film, he might go as far as setting up a suicide . . . it was suicide wasn't it?'

'Yes,' I breathed out slowly. This Danton woman seemed to know all the answers.

'I'll hire you for a week, Mr. Flute, please find out everything you can. Maybe I should have told you a bit more about the characters in question, but I didn't think it would help.'

'Anything helps.' I tried not to sound too tired.

'Oscar is a very odd character and Noelle isn't much simpler. You see,' she said after a significant pause, 'everyone in films knows that Noelle is having an affair with Oscar, but no one really believes it.

15

They're not meant to. Please try again.'

I hung up after saying goodbye and turned round to look at a bunch of reporters who had been listening to my end of the conversation. I smiled at them and showed them my empty glass.

'The first one who fills that up for free gets the story of the year.'

There wasn't a great rush. Two younger reporters dug their hands into their pockets but didn't bring them out again.

'Miss Knowles,' I said in a loud proud voice, 'is not dead.'

No one moved. One of the old hands looked up at me as though he had acute acid indigestion and it was my fault, another smiled sympathetically.

'We know that, you burk,' he said kindly, 'that's why we're here.'

It was now a question of saving face of course. I wasn't used to having a gallery of sharks looking down on me as though I were a complete idiot.

'But you haven't got proof,' I said, all knowing.

'Have you?'

'Yes.'

In the corner of the bar two ten-foot-wide gentlemen had been eyeing me for some time, trying to work out which way I would break easiest. I tried to ignore them.

'What?' a reporter said. He was on the point of buying me a drink.

'Noelle Knowles left the hotel this morning.'

I didn't know for sure. It was a hunch, a far-out bid to get me clear of the place looking as though I was someone well worth knowing. Besides, the information made the two gentlemen in the corner sit up, and that was worth my while because I suspected they worked for Lovaks whom I badly wanted to see.

Like a couple of unlubricated robots they moved across the bar to where I was sitting.

'What paper do you work for?' one of them asked.

'*Time & Life, New York Tribune, l'Aurore, Bognor Regis Observer.* Take your pick.'

'A free lance jerk? Maybe you ought to come upstairs for a minute. Mr. Lovaks would like to see you.'

'I'll be here for the next half hour. He doesn't own everyone, you know, and some of his enemies are always ready to pay more than he can for valuable information.'

I wasn't too sure what I was talking about but it had the desired effect. The two robots left the bar to go to report to their boss and my status was being reassessed by everyone else. Something was happening at last. I turned my back on the company and ordered myself the drink that no one else wanted to buy.

Five minutes later a deep American voice offered me a refill. Oscar Lovaks himself, dressed in a subdued scarlet shirt, white trousers, white baseball cap and thick horn-rimmed glasses. He was putting on a kind and slightly nervous act.

'I, er, would like to have words with you, if you can spare me a minute. I have a room upstairs.'

'So I understand,' I said.

'Maybe, er, you'd like a drink up there. More peaceful.'

'Maybe, er, I would,' I said.

The suite he occupied had three french windows overlooking the sea. The door leading to his bedroom, or maybe Noelle Knowle's suite, was locked and in front of it a chair had been placed to dissuade possible intruders. I sat down on a Louis XVI fauteuil and waited for my host to speak.

For a while he said nothing but wandered about the delicately-furnished room like a beast in the beauty's boudoir. He was a heavily-built man, maybe with hair on his shoulders, had a thick neck, a shorn head, his eyes stared fixedly behind the unbreakable lenses. If he wasn't mad he was probably a genius.

'Like, you boobed, Mister?' he started in traditional style.

'I did?'

'You were meant to keep that little story a secret, weren't you?'

'Was I?'

'Who do you work for?'

'Adam Flute.'

'Never heard of him. What is he, a press agent of some kind?'

'An agent.'

'You've done me a lot of harm, a lot. We were building up to a great story for the weekend ... this'll kill it before Friday's out.'

I nearly felt sorry for him, but not quite. He was lighting a cigar and I thought it so unoriginal.

'You could, of course, say you were wrong, admit you were just shouting your mouth off.'

'Mr. Lovaks,' I started in a slow deliberate way, 'would it give you a great shock if I told you that I had absolutely no idea what was going on and that I am in no way connected with films or the Press?'

Lovaks looked up and studied me for quite a while. He was a pretty pale character so he couldn't go paler if he tried.

'Not in the trade, Dad?'

'Not in the trade.'

'Where are you from then?'

'A finance company maybe? The Inland Revenue? I might be a detective investigating the supposed death of Miss

Knowles?' I said.

'But there's nothing to investigate! All the necessary statements were made before we gave out the news.' He was getting annoyed now. 'Who are you anyway, and what do you want?'

'I don't want anything, you asked me up here.'

'Yeah, yeah. Well, why did you spill the story?'

'No reason, just sudden impulse.'

He breathed out, a long bored sigh which told me that he thought I was a nut.

'No guy goes around messing other people's plans without a reason. You want money?'

The temptation was there, all I had to do was put out my hand, sign a statement that I didn't know what I had been talking about and clear out — but I had my client's welfare to think about.

'Where is Miss Knowles now?' I asked.

'Why should I tell you?'

'That's all I want.'

'If I tell you will you put the Press right? Will you even say you've seen the body?'

'If my name isn't mentioned, yes.'

'O.K. Miss Knowles is back in England. Flew back late last night.'

'So I was right?'

'Yes, you were right.'

'Pretty clever really,' I said to annoy him, then added: 'England is big, where did she go?'

'Before I tell you any more, you tell me who you're working for.'

He was unwrapping a piece of chewing gum from a new packet and popping the stick into his mouth. I handed him my card and watched him read it.

'Private Eye eh? Who's paying you?'

Occasionally I had bright ideas, occasionally I remembered things and used my memory to the best advantage. 'Laminated Wools, Ltd.,' I said.

'Bastards!'

He crossed the room, wrote an address down on a piece of paper and crossed the room again to hand it to me. Noelle Knowles was keeping quiet in a quiet hotel smack in the middle of South Kensington.

'What's the next step?' I asked.

He was showing me the way to the door and not being very friendly.

'You just tell the boys downstairs that you lied and that you've just seen the body.'

'There's a rumour going around that you and Miss Knowles are more than friends.'

'Yeah, well, that's all part of the stunt.'

'She supposedly committed suicide because she couldn't make up her mind who to choose, you or her husband?'

'Something like that.'

'With all this publicity I suppose she then gets a part in the film?' I suggested.

'It's already being written. So you've got what you wanted, so you do your part of the bargain?'

'But it isn't a rumour is it? It's true.'

'You'll find the Press boys downstairs, Flute, hand them your story — anyway you like, maybe you could pretend you're a psychopath or something, it shouldn't be difficult.'

'When are you leaving for England?'

'Goodbye Mr. Flute.'

He had the door open and his hand

was indicating the way out. He'd lived a thousand years this man, he knew all the answers, he was bored with them and was always trying something new to shock, to surprise, to make news.

'When you've finished this particular job,' he suggested, 'you might let me know — I need a bloke like you to keep blokes like you away.'

'I'm expensive.'

'Laminated Wools will pay.'

I hadn't pulled any over his eyes. He knew I wasn't anything to do with the company and he was genuinely uninterested in what I was really doing, providing I didn't bother him any more.

Downstairs I told the barman that I had just seen Miss Knowles, but wasn't sure whether she was alive or dead, would he pass the message on to his journalist friends? He said he would as soon as they returned from the beach. They had all rushed out to see a girl who had been reported as wearing a swimsuit that didn't show her navel. I got myself a taxi and went to Nice Airport.

There was nothing exceptional about the Leamington Residential Hotel except that it was teetotal and the residents had been staying there for the last sixty years. The only occasions of lightheartedness were when a guest departed, usually in a hearse.

The young woman behind the counter, she was fifty-five, smiled at me like any woman of that age smiles at someone else's son.

'Miss Knowles,' I said, and she smiled some more.

'She's just finished dinner and gone up to wash. She'll be down in a few minutes. Whom shall I say?'

'Her brother.'

She gave me an odd look, worried a bit about me, then suggested I might like to sit in the lounge.

Among the dead men who couldn't see the magazines they were reading was an exception to the rule. Her hair was dull brown and as lifeless as the lifeless hair in the TV ads, she was probably forty under the heavy make-up, but she had a fair pair of legs unfortunately sheathed in black woollen stockings. She hugged a shawl round her shoulders and I guessed she was convalescing, but I wanted to sit next to someone who was breathing and who might be able to tell me a little bit about the dump.

'What time do they serve breakfasts here?' I asked as an opening gambit.

She edged a little away from me and pulled her shawl closer to her bosom — which wasn't anything to ignore under the green twinset.

'I like eating breakfast late — saves me buying lunch,' I continued.

She smiled pleasantly enough, but just enough to make me realize she wasn't interested in any of my vices.

I let it go. It was too much trouble and there were other legs in the world. Besides I was waiting to see someone pretty dishy.

She came through the open double doors of the lounge carrying a large volume of Tolstoy's *War and Peace*, Part II. She was about five foot three, wore a navy blue dress and leaned heavily on a stick.

'You wished to see me?' she said in a quivering voice.

'Miss Knowles?' I asked.

'Yes.'

'I think there must be some mistake. You're not the Miss Knowles I was looking for.'

She was disappointed. She had been disappointed all seventy-five years of her life and this was just another one. She walked out of the lounge in the direction of the television room and I felt sorry for her.

'Knowles, I suppose, is a pretty common name,' I said sitting down again next to the mouse. It was warm in the lounge and certainly peaceful enough to think, and that was all I wanted to do.

I hadn't banked on Lovaks sending me to the right address, but I was disappointed. It meant I couldn't charge the Danton woman too much on expenses.

'Maybe you should have asked for her by Christian name as well,' the shawled one suggested, getting friendly.

'Maybe, but I guess she isn't using her

real name anyway.'

She was intrigued by this, I could tell. I was suggesting something sinister, or dramatic and it made the woman's magazine she was reading a little less fictitious.

'What's your name?' I asked suddenly to frighten her.

She hesitated, the pause lengthened, I turned to face her fair and square and watched her mouth open but no words came out.

'Your name?' I repeated.

'Mary Jones.'

She was composed now, calmer, but the load of powder on her forehead had taken a shaking, and the grey eyebrows looked younger than the trace of chalk intended them to be.

'Mary Jones?' I said to myself, slowly, 'I don't think that even a real overdose of sleeping tablets could change your name to Mary Jones, Miss Knowles.'

3

I found it strange that a supposedly up and coming film star should dress up as an old woman and sit among those she imitated for kicks. But then I didn't know Noelle Knowles.

I experienced an embarrassing few minutes when she laughed out loud at the thought of being exposed and even louder at the gaping expressions of the hotel residents. As quietly as I could I suggested we should move elsewhere which remark provided me with a clue to her character.

'In this dump? Brother there isn't even a bar!'

Had I been warned I might have been more careful with her. With the faint smell of alcohol drifting my way I guessed I was in the company of a mild dipso.

I followed Miss Knowles to the lift with the obvious intent to accompany her to her bedroom. The receptionist didn't wink, either she trusted her guest not to indulge in anything too naughty, or she had a clean mind.

The lift travelled pretty fast and took just under five minutes to get to the first floor, as Miss Knowles had pressed the button for the fifth, I engaged her in a dynamic conversation.

'Good journey back from Nice?'

'Yes thank you.'

'Private planes are always a bit tricky I find.'

'Are they.'

'A car brought you straight here from the airfield.'

'Why do you ask, if you know?'

I got a surprise, the top floor of the hotel was different. The lift gates opened out onto a tan carpeted, white walled corridor which led to a wrought iron reinforced glazed glass door. Through it I could discern the shadows of potted plants and a bronze statue or two. A snazzy penthouse, I thought, as unexpected as Miss Knowles's behaviour.

'This way,' she said opening the door as though she owned the place.

The main room had a bay window overlooking the tops of the trees, it had been furnished lavishly with the most acceptable contemporary junk you can get on the market and on the walls I recognized a Cezanne or a Renoir, one of those earth bound Southern Frenchman anyway who spent their time falling in love with olive trees.

I picked up a Venetian three-legged coffee cup and ran my finger over the gold encrustations.

'Don't drop it, they're worth seven guineas each. I bought the whole set in Paris at the Marché au Puces.'

I looked her over, she was standing straighter now and her legs were really something. She didn't look a bit the type to go around flea markets hunting out antiques, but then who did?

'This all your collection?' I asked glancing about the room.

'No. Only the coffee set.'

I wondered whose flat we were in, I could make a guess that it was Lovaks's, but it seemed odd for a film director to be living at the top of a mortuary.

I was following her around hoping she would lead me to one of the other rooms where I might find an opportunity of guessing who the owner was. She led me straight to the bedroom, but I wasn't any the wiser.

There was a double bed with four posts round it, so that you could imagine Queen Elizabeth had slept there. On the walls four old masters of no great reputation hung on gold chains, their value didn't add up to much but they handed the room an atmosphere of stately homes on a plate.

She had started unpacking earlier, but hadn't finished. On the floor, the chairs, the bed itself I had a preview of what she might be wearing for the next few weeks. Two pairs of pyjamas caught my interest, they were made of some plastic material and transparent, on a dresser there were a dozen different foundation creams, five lipsticks, four bottles of scent, six white bras on the floor, two black bras on the door handle, one red stuffed in a slipper, a tube of toothpaste on the washstand right next to an empty bottle of Champagne.

'The bed comfortable?' I asked.

She gave me one of those looks reserved for such remarks. I hadn't meant it that way, I just wanted to know whether she had slept there before.

'Want to try it?' She was busy slapping some make-up remover on her face and it was already improving her looks.

I didn't answer, not wishing to commit myself so early on, and wandered over to the open suitcase on the bed. Inside it were two film scripts. 'LONELY ARE THE DAMNED' both of them were titled, and both of them had a woman's part underlined throughout.

We were moving back into the sitting room now with a white towel rubbing off the greasepaint. At some stage during the proceedings she had managed to whip off her black stockings — I was surprised I hadn't noticed, but then I had been taking in the surroundings.

'Why the astonished expression?' she said suddenly.

'Oh, was it? I was wondering whose apartment this was.'

'The owner of the hotel. Anything else?'

'I'd like to know whether it's true about you and Oscar Lovaks.'

She stopped in front of a gilt mirror and gave me my second surprise of the day. Deftly removing a long pin from somewhere within the bun at the back of her mouse-coloured hay rick, she neatly pulled what turned out to be a wig revealing a sweet head of short-cropped blonde hair. She looked as sexy as if she had got out of a cold bath on a torrid afternoon. I moved a step forward.

'That better?'

'I always fancied old maids myself. But why the disguise in the first place?'

'It's a long story. Maybe you haven't got the time?'

'All the time in the world, blondy.'

She moved with a little swing of the hips to a row of bookshelves, pushed them back to reveal a recess full of bottles, mixed me some affair and handed me the glass.

'What's in this?'

'Nothing you need be frightened of

— I'm drinking the same.'

'Maybe you're immuned.'

She was casting the right sort of spell, switching on some cool music somewhere and making the most of the pink setting sun and not turning on any lights. With a gentle pat at a cushion she suggested I should sit right down next to her on a bed that was called a sofa for decency's sake and I took a sip of her cocktail and felt the pit of my stomach do the twist.

'You haven't answered my question,' I said softly.

'Which was what?'

'Whether Justin knows about you and Oscar Lovaks?'

'Are you working for him?'

It was a question which answered many. With that one short sentence I knew that Lovaks must have contacted her to tell her about me, that she suspected Justin of hiring a Private Eye which, in turn, meant that everything couldn't be too happy between them.

'No, I don't work for him,' I said.

'Who do you work for?'

'Why did you get all dressed up?'

'Boredom, partly, also a determination to play my part well in the film I'm making. I end up as an old archaeologist, thought I'd get into the skin of the old dear.'

'Method,' I said.

'Who do you work for?' she asked again.

'Lovaks.' It was just to muddle her up.

'What?'

'Oscar Lovaks, he makes films.'

'I know! *He* hired *you*?'

'That's what I said.'

'But what for?'

'To see that you behave yourself.'

'Doesn't he trust me?'

'Should he?'

'I've done everything he's told me.'

'Really?' I paused to give her one of those irritating sexy all knowing looks, then added, 'Including doping my drink?'

I had started feeling drowsy and I could taste a familiar bitterness on the roof of my palate. I had been put to sleep before.

She didn't answer me directly but thought carefully about what she should

36

say. I was toying with the idea of casually dropping my glass on the carpet but didn't. Instead I looked at her troubled brow, her large blue too innocent eyes, her slightly upturned nose, her sensuous mouth. She was about twenty-three I reckoned and as experienced as they come at that age.

'Yes,' she said at last, 'I did dope your drink. He asked me to . . . but why?'

'But why what? Why should he want me doped?'

'Yes! If you're working for him?'

'Just to see how far he can trust you. See how far you'll go along with his crazy publicity ideas.'

'You think they're crazy?'

She was worried about it. This was the one thing she was really worried about. She was being a good girl, because it probably said she had to in her contract, but she was worried about breaking the law and having to do unpleasant things to nice, pleasant people like me.

'He's gone a bit too far this time,' I said, 'doping his own staff, but that's none of my business.'

'Did he tell you he was coming here tonight?'

'Mmmm,' I said not committing myself.

She glanced across the room at a large carriage clock on the false chimney piece.

'What time did he tell you he'd be here? Within the hour?'

'Mmmm,' I said again, then to liven things up, 'What did you put in this drink?'

'A white powder he gave me.'

'How much?' There was anxiety in my voice.

'About half a teaspoonful.'

'Half a teaspoonful!! Are you trying to kill me?'

Already my eyes were looking all round the room and I was finding it difficult to breathe. She was really worried.

'Was it too much?'

'I'll be out for a month, if not longer. I have a weak heart . . . you see.' My eyes were closing slowly now and my breathing was even more irregular.

'Isn't there something I can do?'

'Water . . . lots of water, it's the only thing.'

She left the room in a flash and came back with a tall glass of water with a couple of ice cubes floating on the top.

'Would coffee help?'

'Coffee would.'

There was no kitchen in the penthouse, just a cupboard with an icebox, and a telephone that rang a bell directly in the ear of some poor cook who lived in the basement. Noelle picked up the receiver, asked for a large cup of blackest coffee, then we both heard the lift gates close and looked at each other.

'Your lover,' I said. 'I'll make like I'm cold.' So saying I let myself slide back on the three comfortable cushions on the sofa and closed my eyes.

The door of the penthouse opened and I heard the Knowles girl say something like 'Sshh!' As there was no sound after that for what seemed like an hour I opened one eye very slowly and saw the two of them in one of the hottest clinches I had seen for a long time. Lovaks was hungry for this short cropped young blonde and she didn't behave as though she'd been fed recently either. They released each other after two minutes and came into the sitting room.

'How long has he been out?'

'Not long.'

'Everything go according to plan?'

'Yes, I met him downstairs.'

'Downstairs? I told you not to show yourself!'

'No one recognized me. It was fun anyway. I looked just like one of the guests.'

'You been at the bottle again?'

'Only bubbly. It's all I've got when you're not there.'

'Sweety . . . you'll get into trouble one of these days. You have such crazy ideas when you're under the influence. Lay off it for a year will you, for my sake.'

'For you, anything.'

'Have you packed?'

'Not yet.'

'I'll give you a hand, we haven't much time.'

'Why what's the hurry?'

I had my eyes so firmly shut that I

wasn't too sure where they were. They were moving around a good deal and maybe were talking just inside the bedroom.

'Sleeping beauty may have tipped off Justin where you're hiding.'

'Why should he do that?'

'Why shouldn't he?'

The silence that followed told me she was working things out. If she lost her temper I was a little bit vulnerable. I clenched my teeth and waited.

'He's not working for you then?'

'No, of course not! I don't know who he's working for, he's just a smarter type of freelance reporter who needs to learn a few things — which this knockout stuff ought to do. By the time he wakes up it'll be too late . . . What are you doing?'

Luckily she chose to use a large volume of Boccaccio's *Decameron* on the back of my head and, being bound of supple leather, failed to knock me out, though I must admit it gave me one big shock. My backbone, just where it's fixed to the head, took most of the impact and sent a nasty sensation right down my spine. But

I survived enough to open my eyes and stare coldly at Lovaks who was perplexed by the whole sequence of events.

'Are you nuts Noelle, what are you doing?'

It was because the volume was numbered and watermarked that he stopped her having a second crack at me, otherwise I would have had a bad episode of concussion.

'He told me he was working for you!'

'So you didn't give him the stuff?'

'Yes — but then some water so it wouldn't take effect. Now he knows about us!'

I didn't get to my feet in time, and I didn't think he had it in him. His left fist came at me at an odd angle, blocking the light and making it very easy to parry. It was the right that I didn't see at all, not until I woke up some time later and remembered it as I felt that sensitive part of my jaw just below the ear where it swells up if you hit hard enough to knock a man cold.

★　★　★

From my watch I calculated that I had been asleep about two hours. With the remains of the powder and the K.O., my brain wasn't too keen to let me get up and walk the streets so I kept myself under observation for another half hour.

It was dark and I was alone, whether anyone had come into the penthouse and seen me there sprawled on the floor or not I had no idea, but the flat was tidy, tidy in a way that told me it was pointless looking in the bedroom for Miss Knowles's clothes.

Being a sleuth of the first order, however, I padded around and opened a few drawers and cupboards to find out if I could confirm the owner's identity. It took me two seconds to get a definite answer.

In the small bathroom, in one of the cupboards, I found an emergency stock of shaving equipment which had been used. In one of the cupboards in the bedroom I found three men's suits which would have fitted Lovaks perfectly, and in one of the drawers of the bedside tables, I found an old photograph of my dear client, Zeelah

Danton. 'To My Darling Oscar,' it read and was dated 2.12.52. Some people never bothered to open drawers and tidy up after a broken marriage.

Downstairs in the morgue, which was as dark as any self-respecting teetotal houses should be, I found my way out by unlocking the six devices which had been screwed into the door to keep the inmates from straying. I didn't have the time to find out how Lovaks fitted in this set-up but I guessed that some rich aunt had left him the whole building in a will. It was a pleasantly secretive place for a bachelor film director anyway.

★ ★ ★

Zeelah Danton lived in a small terrace house West of Westminster, near Vincent Square. The bricks were black but it had a Royal Blue door with a brass knocker representing a yawning lion which had been lacquered so that no one had to clean its teeth every week. I used the lower part of its jaw to bang loudly enough to wake up everyone in the district. I was in that sort of mood. It was just past eleven-thirty but a light was still on in the front room.

She wasn't expecting any visitors and wasn't too pleased to see me, but she let me in. She was wearing some faded kimono affair which she allowed herself to wander about the house in. It had seen better days and probably had been seen by a good many admirers.

'I thought you might have kept normal office hours as far as your clients were concerned,' she said.

'I would if I had the time, unfortunately I may have to fly off somewhere and thought I'd better get your approval first. It might be New York which could set you back a few hundred.'

She led me into her bijoux sitting room and suggested I should sit down, offered me a cigarette and a nightcap. Her tots of whisky weren't mean and I was glad of the refreshment.

Before calling on her I had been back to my flat and looked through a couple of old editions of *Spotlight*, the actors' casting directory. I had a number of these odd reference books left me by my crazy Uncle and I had to admit they occasionally came in handy.

Zeelah Danton occupied a whole page in the 'Leading and Younger Leading' section. She had made two films in the last four years and was one of those beauties that had never quite made the top but had managed to earn a good living by slipping into a typecast character which was in regular demand. She was the sophisticated stockbroker's wife who either took to the bottle or a French lover.

'So what did you find out during your little holiday in the South of France?' she asked, warming up to an argument with her erring husband type part. She was settling down nicely on a miniature chaise longue opposite me.

'Oscar Lovaks is having an affair with Noelle Knowles.'

'Where?'

'Where?' I was surprised by the question. 'I don't think they have a set place, if that's what you mean. An affair is a bit tangible . . . if you know what I mean.'

'You have proof?'

'I saw them getting into a pretty amorous clinch.'

'A what?'

'I saw them embracing each other passionately.'

'Oh.' She seemed disappointed.

'I wasn't able to follow them into the bedroom,' I said to cheer her up.

'Did they go in?'

'No. That's why I wasn't able to follow them.'

She didn't think my humour funny, but smiled politely. For a while she watched me smoke my cigarette, I told myself it was admiration.

'They've gone on somewhere else.'

'Where were they?'

'A penthouse flat in Leamington Square.'

'Oh, that dreadful place above an old folks' home, poor girl, I would have thought he could do better than that now!'

'The Leamington Residential Hotel, you know it?'

'We spent the first night of our

honeymoon there, thank you. The place belonged to one of Oscar's innumerable aunts. I didn't know he still had it, the idiot.'

I finished my whisky and tinkled the ice about at the bottom of the glass. My guess had been right, but it wouldn't bring me in any money.

'Could you do one more thing for me?'

'I'm at your service, you're paying me.'

'Would you find Justin and tell him what's happening.'

'I can do, but why don't you tell him yourself?'

'He'd think it was sour grapes.'

'Which of course it isn't?' I gave her a long critical look but she didn't react. Instead she thought, carefully, for a long time.

'Tell him what you've told me, that you saw them together in the Hotel. Then let me know what he said. That's all.'

'Don't you think he already knows?'

'Justin? No, I shouldn't think so, he's too proud a man to even imagine that a woman might be interested in someone else. You just do that little job and then you can send me your account.'

'I'd prefer to have something now,' I said to surprise her. I didn't mean it, but I just wanted to know if she would be ready to fish up for all the hard work I'd done.

She stalled, sat up, looked worried, concerned, troubled, did a bit of unscripted method acting then dreamed up this lunatic story about her not having her cheque book handy.

'It doesn't matter,' I said with an irritating smile, all knowing. 'But until I have some sort of advance you understand that I can't really consider you as my client — should anything happen.'

'What could happen?'

We were standing up now and about to move to the door. I was enjoying this bit of melodrama.

'Mr. Joyce might ask me who I was and what I was doing, poking my nose into his business. He might ask me who hired me. Mr. Lovaks might want to buy some information . . . '

'I can let you have £50 now. The rest on Monday.'

'That should cover the French trip, anyway,' I said.

I smiled some more when she went to a small bureau and found, quite by accident, her cheque book. She obviously had enough money to live on comfortably if she didn't indulge in any extra extravagant expenses. I was obviously going to be one of those expenses, but I figured that somehow in her life I was worth it.

'I've never paid a man before,' she said handing me the little piece of mauve paper with her autograph on it.

I was about to make the appropriate remark when I heard a sound just beyond the door. Zeelah Danton didn't hear it, or pretended not to, but to me the gentle scraping of soft leather on polished floor meant that someone was around listening.

I gave Zeelah a long look, which she tried to puzzle out while I listened some more, then when I was quite sure that someone was in the hallway I spun round, made a grab for the door knob and pulled the door wide open.

She looked about fifteen, had long

blonde hair down to her shoulders and some way down her back, and smiled with wide open innocent eyes.

'April! What *are* you doing?' Mother Zeelah was genuinely surprised and furious.

'Listening. I wanted to know who your latest gigolo was.'

4

Gigolo Flute left the small terrace house as discreetly as he could after taking a good long look at the blonde daughter.

I had recognised her the moment I had seen her. She had made one film, was now being promoted as England's own home-grown Lolita and her name — her stage name — was April Mundy.

She was the offspring of the Zeelah-Oscar Lovaks union, and though such a talented pedigree could well have been plastered all over her publicity throwouts, it had never been mentioned.

I climbed into my Porsche Super 90 and waved at her frowning face framed in the top floor bedroom window. She didn't wave back because I wasn't supposed to be able to see her. She was very sweet though, and very attractive, like her mother, it was a shame that there wasn't another female in the family halfway between them, age wise.

Back at the flat I mixed myself a strong cocktail of milk and chocolate powder, simmered it on the stove for a few minutes and was about to slip my tired feet into bed when the telephone rang. The few friends I had never rang me this late, so I picked up the receiver with some misgivings. I said nothing but just listened.

'Mr. Flute? I thought I'd ring to apologise for the interruption — she's getting a little out of hand, success has gone to her head.'

'Doesn't it go to everyone's?' I said, for something to say.

I gradually inserted myself between the white sheets of my double bed and sank deep down into its cold loneliness. Soon it would be warm with me radiating heat, meanwhile I tucked the receiver between my ear and the pillow, lit myself a cigarette and listened. It was going to be a long conversation.

'You only rang up to apologize?' I asked.

'No . . . I rang up to tell you a bit more about Justin, and why I want you to tell him what's happening.'

'I know why.'

'Do you?'

'You're just being bitchy.'

'I don't know why, Mr. Flute,' she said after a pause. 'But I can't get annoyed with you, maybe it's your face, or your illogical way of working. You're just a big joke.'

I was hurt, of course, just about as hurt as she was. I said nothing, but drew on my cigarette and tried to look more serious. Into a telephone receiver it's never very easy.

'Are you there?'

'Yes, I'm smarting under the insult,' I said.

'I'm sorry.'

'So am I. You were saying?' The dialogue was taking an amorous turn, I didn't like it, though her voice was gentleness itself to any man alone in a double bed.

'I'd like to talk to you at length about my motives for hiring you, but meanwhile will you please see Justin?'

'Of course.'

'Do you know where to find him?'

'Down in Cannes, I expect. That's where he was this morning.'

'He'll be in London tomorrow, at the BBC Television Centre, rehearsing a new play.'

'I see. He gets around.'

'Most famous actors do. He is in great demand. Some actors make a film, appear in television and act on the stage every night during some seasons!'

'I see,' I said again, feeling sorry for all overworked actors.

'You'll have to choose the right moment to see him because April will also be there, she's in the play too and I wouldn't like her to . . . '

'Eavesdrop again.'

'No.'

'Then maybe it might be wiser if I waited till the rehearsal was over?'

'I'm trying to cut down on my expenses Mr. Flute. He'll be flying back to the South of France afterwards.'

'Busy man!'

'As I said, he's famous, at the moment.'

I thought of Justin Joyce, of the tired

face, the creased features, the unsober eyes and smoked-out lungs. People were worshipping this man for his youth and vigour. I loved the honesty of the film business.

'I'll see him on the set then, when no one's around. I'll tell him I'm some sort of Press guy. Leave it to me.'

'Perhaps we could have dinner afterwards,' she said in that deep smooth voice of hers.

'Yes, yes of course.' She was a client after all.

'But if you see me at the centre, you won't recognize me, will you?'

'No. Are you likely to be there?'

'I'm taking a small part in the same play.'

She hung up on the dramatic exit line and left me with the receiver hurting my left ear. I put it back in its cradle, stubbed out my cigarette and switched off the light. Under the criss-cross reflections of the street lights on the ceiling I thought about the whole set-up and about Zeelah Danton. She had plenty reasons for feeling bitter, having to take a small part in the same play as her up and coming teenage daughter and her ex-husband. I turned over and stopped thinking about her, instead I thought of the glass of hot chocolate which I had left in the kitchen and which would now be at just the right temperature to drink. I thought about it, but I didn't get up.

★ ★ ★

The value of an expensive sports car is not only in the comfort of the driving but in the prestige it gives you, especially when dealing with the funny little men who are put in uniforms by a public body. I knew my Porsche wouldn't impress anyone so I hired myself a small vermilion Aston-Martin DB4 and sailed through the BBC Centre gates without being stopped. I parked the throbbing machine where it said 'No Parking', ignored the doubtful looks that I was given and walked straight through the double glass swing doors of the reception hall.

In this airline terminal atmosphere I waited for a while at the reception desk where four overworked girls were contacting every person that was unavailable. I looked up at the mural while I waited. It didn't do anything to me except worry me about how it was put up there. Then the girl smiled and asked me who I wanted.

'Dick Forsythe,' I lied. I knew how to deal with such situations.

She turned up a large index file, looked for the name 'Forsythe' found it and looked puzzled.

'We have a Hugh Forsythe, is that him?'

'No,' I said. I lit a cigarette, looked impatient and even more important.

'I won't keep you a moment.'

'He's over here for a while from NBC, New York.'

'Oh, do you know what department?'

'Documentaries. Look, I know my way around, I'll find him.'

Without waiting I gave her a big smile and headed for the lifts. She wasn't supposed to let me go, but I knew she wouldn't get the sack for not calling the commissionaire. They never sack anybody at the BBC, not even the house detectives.

I pressed the first floor button in the aluminium cage and seconds later walked out onto an antiseptic linoleumed corridor. I guessed that most of the studios would be on the ground floor so made my way down again by the stairs. No one seemed to be following me.

In Studio C I found the rehearsal I wanted, the play was called *Death, My Secret* and right then looked pretty dead. I joined a group of nonentities who were sitting around looking as though they might be needed and watched the slow progress of the play taking shape.

April Mundy was lying on her stomach on the floor supposedly reading a book. She was dressed in faded jeans, a short white shirt and no shoes. Her sister — her TV sister that is — was reclining on a sofa two feet away supposedly listening to some jazzy quartet on a small transistor. The radio set was a sweet little machine with a blue dial and little red knobs, but it wasn't half as sweet as the long haired brunette who had a slightly oriental look about the eyes and a figure made to drive the cameramen scatty.

'Who's the doll on the sofa?' I asked a young actor who was so bored he'd obviously seen Larry Olivier in the same play at Chichester.

'Pascale Anjoux. France's answer to our own little April Mundy!'

'Any good?'

'In bed? Don't know. Don't go in for that sex myself. Do you?'

'Yes.'

'Crazy!'

He gave me the once over, liked the way I held my cigarette or the slant of my nose or something, but gave up whatever idea he had entertained.

'She's a good little actress,' he said, answering my question. 'Talent, the critics call it nowadays. It's a new gimmick. I marry her in the second act.'

'Congratulations,' I said.

Justin Joyce was nowhere to be seen, nor was Zeelah Danton, neither of them were in this scene which concerned a catty little argument between the two sisters about some boy.

I couldn't pretend, like my actor friend, that I wasn't interested in the two little nymphettes. They were the most exciting performers I had seen for a long time, especially when they broke into the unscripted dialogue that shocked most of the technicians, from whom they had picked up most of the words.

The producer, a tall lean man with sad eyebrows, who had no desire to go to bed with either of them, was getting the worst of it. He was telling them that they should really be angry with each other and not just insulting, but they both favoured the sullen looks, the pouts, the long silences.

'This play runs for forty-five minutes, not a hundred and sixty!'

'Oh that was such a clever remark, anyone would think you write the script!' It was young Pascale getting up off the sofa and looking really bored.

'*Wrote!* Not write! If you're going to act with me you'll have to speak better English than that!' April was on her knees now and feeling very testy.

'Can *you* speak *French*?'

'Here we go again!' The last remark

came from an elderly man behind me who had come into the studio without me noticing. He was obviously an executive of some sort because he stepped right over the producer's head and got the two girls in a referee's pow-wow. The producer just stopped and watched, wiped his fevered brow, sighed and looked around at the technicians. No one thought much of him so he only got sympathy from me.

After about five minutes the executive took the producer aside and after another five minutes someone said something in an inaudible voice and everyone left the studio.

My actor friend slid off his table, admired the way I tied my shoelaces and batted his eyelids once or twice.

'Like to have tea with me, in the canteen?'

'Not today, lover boy,' I said, and watched him mince out of the studio.

I was alone, with three arc lamps which suddenly went out and one 300-watt bulb stuck high up in the ceiling among the gantries, chains, booms, electric cables and lifting devices which helped to decorate the place.

I read the big notice which told me I wasn't allowed to smoke, stubbed out my cigarette on the concrete floor and made a move towards the exit. Maybe Justin was in the canteen having a cup of tea.

I pulled open the thick soundproof door and found myself facing a young girl on the other side. She looked at me carefully, a little nervously, then plucked up enough courage to ask me the question which was disturbing her.

'You're not by chance Mr. Adam Flute? Excuse me asking.'

'Yes, I am,' I said.

'Oh, at last! I've been looking for you everywhere. A Mr. Dick Forsythe is on the telephone, he wishes to speak to you.'

'Mr. Dick Forsythe?' I repeated. 'Who's he then?' It could be coincidence, there might be a man bearing such a name, I had chosen it myself because it sounded right. Yet there seemed to be a catch in it somewhere.

'Who is Mr. Forsythe?' I asked.

The girl didn't know. She'd never

heard of the man but then she hadn't heard of lots of people. Mr. Bartok's office had rung asking her to find Mr. Flute for Mr. Forsythe, and she had done just that. Mr. Bartok, she explained, was head of all TV productions. I took my imaginary hat off.

The girl led me down a short corridor, up some stone steps, left then right, then down another corridor till we reached a small office which had a window overlooking a garden roof. There was nothing special in the office except the blue curtains, the two easy chairs, the thick pile carpet, the walnut desk and the telephone with its receiver sleeping on the blotting pad.

'This it?'

'Yes,' she said. She was blinking nervously and didn't know whether to leave me alone or stay in the room. I made it easy for her, I smiled. Maybe the receptionist downstairs had reported my unconventional entry into the studios to one of the detectives. Maybe this was a trap.

'Flute?' The receiver said to me when I put it to my ear.

'Yes?'

'Studio 5, meet me in the monitoring room, a word with you might do us both a lot of good.'

The other end rang off and I smiled some more. The girl blinked, straightened her skirt and sat down. She didn't know how lucky she was sitting there behind her typewriter. At five she'd be off home. Where would I be?

★   ★   ★

I got to Studio 5 without too much difficulty, pushed open the soundproof door, ignored the set that was all lit up behind the props and made my way up the short steep steps that led to the monitoring room.

There were three deep swivel arm-chairs, the main monitoring panel of miniature screens and behind them a sheet of plate glass overlooking the studio.

I could have seen him in the flesh if I'd looked through the window but I saw him first on the monitoring screens. The three cameras in the studio were switched on and focussed on him, they were all good clear pictures, one a close-up, one a medium shot, one a high angled long shot. He was lying on the floor, spreadeagled on his back, smack in the centre of his chest was the hilt of an Early German broadsword and on his face a pained expression. From experience I knew he was dead.

5

It was the close-up picture of the corpse in Camera 3 that was really the best. The face was upside down, the eyes wide open and the tongue uncomfortably jammed between clenched teeth. Not satisfied with the black and white reproduction of my friend, I ventured down into the studio to have a better look at him.

Studios are soundproof and sound-proof places have an eerie feeling about them. You can stand quite still and listen to the silence hurting your eardrums which makes things uncanny. With a dead body and a bit of vibrantly fresh blood staring you in the face the atmosphere doesn't get any gayer.

I knew that sooner or later someone would come along and see me looking at the dead body and take it upon themselves to accuse me of the crime. It wasn't exactly by accident that I was right there on the spot, someone had very cleverly followed all my movements since I had entered the Centre, someone had manoeuvred me into this incriminating position.

Just to make sure that the killer hadn't left any obvious clues I bent down over the remains of Justin Joyce and examined him very carefully.

Somehow he had lost his appeal, maybe it was that dead look in his eyes with the jelly white of the cornea staring up at me, or just me feeling squeamish. Had it been anyone else the situation might have been simpler, but killing such a famous man right in the middle of the BBC Centre was asking for publicity. I couldn't help thinking of my friend Oscar Lovaks.

I backed away from the corpse and, ignoring the rules, lit up a cigarette. As I inhaled my first puff I got the feeling that I was being watched. There was no one in the studio but me, the dead man and the three cameras, and it was camera 2 with its bright red light and shining lens that made me realize I had probably been watched all the time I had been in the studio.

I turned, looked the lens straight in the optical nerve then stepped out of its focal range. As I did so two technicians came into the studio and stopped in their tracks.

'I wouldn't come any further if I were you,' I said. 'In fact, one of you might be good enough to ring the police.'

'Why, what's happened, mate?'

'Someone's met with an accident. Mr. Joyce.'

'Is that a fact?'

'I'll go, Bert.'

Within ten seconds the studio door was jammed with technicians wanting to see what had happened. I tried to hold them back but had no authority to do so and as I had no intention of letting anyone know that I was around I backed into the mêlée of actors and secretaries, assistant producers and electricians and let everyone discover for themselves how lurid a genuine crime could look.

Unnoticed I slipped away from the studio floor and walked up the familiar stairs to the monitoring room. It was empty but for the soundless activities of the screens. I watched as one by one the curious went up to the corpse, pretending they weren't morbidly interested, then coming away with a sick look on their faces. I watched them all closely, fascinated, the BBC had never produced a programme like it.

Two policemen and a plain clothes man suddenly came into view, they could have been actors from another set but the way they cleared the floor could only mean they were the real thing.

A space was made round the victim and the plain clothes man crouched down to examine the murder weapon more closely. He called over his shoulder to someone, then took a good long look at the surroundings.

It was interesting to see a fellow detective doing his bit, he narrowed his eyes as he looked at the cameras then stepped closer to the one that was giving me his picture.

Pulling up a chair to enjoy the rest of the performance I was disturbed by two men who came up the stairs. One was the producer, the other the studio manager.

Both were chewing their nails and looking really worried.

They stopped in the doorway and looked at me in surprise. They didn't know who was in charge anymore and didn't want to risk annoying anyone.

'Come in,' I said. 'And please close the door.'

They did as they were asked, the voice of authority I used would have made them take off their caps if they had had any.

'I'm a detective and I just want to watch what goes on, if I may, please sit down.'

'Would you . . . like the sound? The microphones are probably working.'

The studio manager leaned over me, flicked back one of the switches, turned a knob and fiddled some more. Very loud, very clear the conversation of two or three people came over.

'Where's the microphone situated?' I asked.

'In the far corner, you can't see it on the monitor, but if you look out of the . . . '

'No. Just stay seated, I don't want anyone to know we're up here.'

'Do you think it could be suicide?' It was a girl's voice.

'Suicide? How do you commit suicide with a sword like that? Use your head! Honestly! Old Justin wasn't a contortionist you know.'

'It's nothing to joke about.'

'I'd like to know who did it.'

I glanced at the producer and his manager. They smiled nervously, it was the remark of the year!

'He had enough enemies.'

'Yeah? What do you know about it?'

'April will be involved.'

'And Pascale.'

'Why her?'

'Why not?'

'Sshh! Here's Zeelah!'

It was better than any show he had ever produced and the producer leaned further forward. The tension was terrific. 'There's Zeelah!' he said to the studio manager. 'Maybe I should go and have a word with her.'

'Maybe you should stay here,' I said.

'What's so important about her anyway?'

'She was married to Mr. Joyce, the victim.'

'Was she?'

Zeelah walked straight into the hands of the plain clothes man who was by now surrounded by policemen. Notebooks were being displayed all over the place, the screen was getting even more crowded and there was so much noise that the microphone wasn't revealing anything of value.

'Would she have had a motive?' I asked over my shoulder.

'What, to kill Justin? . . . No! She's still mad about him.'

'Is she?'

'So they say. Been trying hard to get him back ever since they parted.'

'Hardly likely to kill him then,' I said. 'Any more names you could mention which might cast some light on the subject?'

'Well, there's his present wife of course, Noelle Knowles. I heard it said that she and Mr. Lovaks . . . '

'I know about that, but Miss Knowles

isn't here at the studios is she?'

They were going to say something but didn't because the door swung open and one of the plain clothes men we had seen starring on the screen appeared in real life.

He was tall, in his early forties, had a pale complexion, looked as though he might smoke a pipe, held a soft felt hat, wore a Burberry, grey flannel trousers and brown polished shoes.

'I'm Detective Inspector Furrows,' he said. Behind him a younger man of the same school was casting a professional eye over everything. This was the sort of case he had joined the police force for, television studio murders, sexy looking birds in tights walking round the corridors, bright lights, rowdy music. It was all very thrilling.

'I would just like your names please and your movements during the last hour.'

The producer and the studio manager both gave their names and told the men they had been in the canteen, and a hundred other tea drinkers could prove it.

I told them my name was Adam Flute, that I was a Private Detective, that I had been alone with the body about ten minutes before anyone else and that I had no one to prove it. I could, however, probably help them with their enquiries.

Furrows let the producer and the manager go and suggested I should accompany his sergeant to a police car where I could answer a few questions without interruption.

The walk from the monitoring room to the police car in the driveway outside provided three newspaper reporters with the story that someone had been detained. Luckily no one took pictures, but in the crowd just outside the studio I caught sight of Zeelah. The look she gave me made me think she suspected me of the murder. I only hoped she realized that this would add an extra bit onto her bill. 'Public humiliation suffered in course of investigation — £90.' I would have only made it eighty if she had smiled at me, or something.

There were two police cars, one black Jaguar Mark II with the blue bobble light on its roof, the other a burgundy red MG Magnet saloon which could have belonged to anyone. This was Furrows's car equipped with one telephone on the left of the back seat.

A policeman opened the door for me and I looked around to see if anyone was watching, this surely would be proof enough that I was assisting the police and not being arrested. But no one was looking in my direction, they were all staring at two uniformed men who were pulling a stretcher out of an ambulance.

Furrows kept me waiting fifteen minutes during which time I chatted about cricket scores to the driver, observed Zeelah Danton leaving by taxi unaccompanied, saw her daughter leaving five minutes later with two other girl actresses and caught sight of the French Anjoux nymph cadging a lift off one of the more male type actors.

Apart from them a multitude of others left, but they didn't interest me. Any one of them could be the murderer but I wasn't concerned with that. All I wanted to do was clear my name with Furrows, get the police out of my hair, get my money from Dame Danton and find a less complicated case. Murder was best left to the organized boys to detect, I was best suited to retrieving erring wives, depraved husbands or sex mad Pomeranians.

Furrows came at the tail end of the general exodus and was followed by the two stretcher bearers with their new but lifeless cargo. In silence a morbid crowd watched them loading the six feet of rigor mortis, that would no longer thrill feminine audiences, into their white van. Without ceremony they pushed the stretcher in, slammed the door shut and drove off ringing their little bell for bravado. It excited a couple of girls and gave the cameramen a sense of drama.

Detective Inspector John Furrows was young to be in the position he was. Either he was intelligent or knew someone influential high up in the force, whichever way he had got to the top he had a certain amount of power and I would have to be nice to him. I smiled when he got into the back of the car next to me, and he smiled back. We were going to be buddies, I could tell.

'This is going to be a sticky one,' he said, offering me a Woodbine.

'Yes?'

'Film star murdered with a bloody great sword at the BBC Centre? The papers will go mad, it'll mean more ulcers and another fortnight of sleepless nights.'

He was going grey at the temples, had greyish eyebrows, his face was a bit creased, but he looked healthier than Justin had looked alive. Maybe he wanted my sympathy.

'No clues?' I asked.

'Too early to say. The main thing was to get a few photographs and the body out. What do you know about the set-up?'

'Very little.'

'Are you working?'

'Yes.'

'Your client involved?'

'Connected.'

'Who?'

'My client? I can't tell you that.'

'Oh now! Let's not have any of this so-called professional etiquette. A man's been brutally murdered today and I want to know who did it by this time tomorrow. I'll find out who your client is sooner or later, so the sooner I know from you the quicker you'll be free of me and my boys and the quicker everyone will be happy.'

'I'll tell you his name as soon as I've spoken to him.' I said I wanted time to think before getting more involved. 'I feel I should at least warn him that I'm going to mention him to you.'

'That's fair. Can you see him soon?'

'The moment you let me go.'

The way he was hiding a smile behind the inhaling of his cigarette told me I had made him very happy. These Private boys are a joke, he was thinking, giving away within seconds their client's gender. I smiled behind my cigarette too, but didn't let him see.

'Can you tell me anything about Justin's background? Family, anything like that?'

'Not much. He was married twice, his first wife was a woman older than himself, an actress called . . . Sonia

Stanton . . . name like that. His second wife, his widow, is Noelle Knowles.'

'She's the girl who was supposed to have committed suicide yesterday in the South of France?'

'Yes.'

'Do you know anything about this suicide?'

'She's alive. It was all a publicity gimmick — it misfired I think.'

'But in misfiring still made the headlines?'

'Yes.'

'Can't help feeling there's a connection between both events. Anything else?'

'Not that I can think of.'

'What were you doing in the studio then?'

'Looking for someone. It was an unfortunate coincidence that I happened to be the first to find Joyce.'

'Why?'

'Because I don't expect you to believe in such a coincidence.'

'I might if I knew your reason for being in the studio. Who were you looking for?'

'A girl, called Pascale Anjoux,' I lied.

'Why were you looking for her?'

I gave him a look, the sort of look one tough guy gives another tough guy when talking about a projected affair in Brighton. He didn't register it but looked straight through me.

'Why were you looking for her?'

'I wanted to ask her out to dinner.'

He believed me, or at least pretended to. He stubbed his cigarette out in the ashtray that hung on the back of the driver's seat and thought for a bit.

'I'll have to question pretty well all the cast and the technicians in the Centre, a small job! If you could see your client and explain the situation as soon as possible I'd be most grateful. With your help I could probably solve this business very quickly.'

I opened the door on my side and started getting out, as I turned to say goodbye, I also said something else. 'I'm going straight to my flat and from there I'll ring him. I won't be meeting him anywhere secret.'

'Why are you telling me this?'

'It would be a waste of time having me followed.'

I slammed the door on his smile and without hurrying, so that everyone could see I was free of handcuffs, ball and chain, prison uniform, I crossed the tarmac to my car. Calmly I got into the convertible, switched on the engine, backed elegantly into the drive and shot off at a speed which could have got me arrested on the spot.

Back at the flat I mixed myself a lime juice and soda, added a dab of ice-cream from the refrigerator and walked out on to the balcony to look at London life going on below. I sat down on the edge of the wall, ignored the fact that if I lost my balance I'd fall sixty-two feet to a concrete death and gave myself the once over.

Putting myself on an imaginary psy-chiatrist's couch inside a confessional box I asked myself a few pertinent questions. My problem was that I hadn't told Furrows I had been hired by Zeelah Danton but I didn't know why I hadn't told him.

It wasn't loyalty to my client, nor a perverted desire to complicate the police's work either — I genuinely liked helping the poor slobs. It wasn't money or sex, because at first sight Miss Danton didn't display too much of either, though if Freud had had a hand in asking me questions I dare say he would have found an Oedipus complex lurking around somewhere. If it was her sex appeal, that gave me this protective instinct, I would have to be very careful what I was doing. She was at least forty-two, still very attractive admittedly, her legs were good, she dressed well, but then clothes usually came off. She had of course a pretty daughter — at which thought I bit right through a chunk of ice-cream.

April Mundy, sixteen. Was I man enough to admit to myself that she had been the cause of my troubled inner self? Until I knew exactly where she figured in the Justin murder, I was going to keep her family right out of Furrows's way.

The problem solved, I wiped my finger round the inside of the glass to get out all the remains of the curdled ice-cream, and listened to the telephone ringing as I licked my sticky finger.

'Don't say who you are,' I said lifting

the receiver. 'The line may be tapped.'

'Oh!' She didn't have to say any more, the deep tremor in her voice was instantly recognizable, it was Zeelah.

'You want to speak to me urgently?'

'Yes.'

'I'll meet you in half an hour in the same place I met you last night. O.K.?'

She paused a moment to work that one out, then agreed. I put down the receiver and complimented myself on having had the presence of mind to impress her. I doubted very much whether the police would bother, so early on, to tap my line.

★ ★ ★

There was no one out in the street outside the block of flats. Either Furrows was short of men, or he trusted me, in which case he was a fool. Boldly I hailed a taxi, gave him Zeelah's address and watched out of the back window all the way there to see if I was being followed. No one acted suspiciously, I was safe.

She looked pretty anxious when she opened the door, and closed it quickly in case neighbours were looking.

'Any visitors?'

'Not so far.'

'The story hasn't got around yet, but it will. The Press boys are the people you'd better watch. You wanted to speak to me.'

'I'm leaving for the South of France, as soon as I can.'

'Is that wise?'

'You mentioned the Press yourself.'

'But the police are more important and they'll . . . '

'Suspect me? You've told them, then, that you were working for me?' Her look was one of utter despair.

'Certainly not. I don't do that sort of thing. You paid me an advance, remember? That's like a contract.'

'Then I've nothing to worry about.'

'You were Justin's first wife and you were near the scene of the murder, that's all you have to worry about.'

'Are you sure it was murder?'

I looked at her the way I look at people when they are stalling for time.

'If you want to get away before the news breaks I suggest you ring up

Scotland Yard and ask them whether you should see anyone before you go. If they know where they can get you and you cooperate, they won't make any difficulties.'

'Will they let me go?'

'They'll ask you a few questions, that's all.'

'What about you? Won't they ask you a few questions too? You were at the scene of the murder as well.'

'I can look after myself. Just tell me what you're liable to tell them.'

'I'll tell them the truth. That I was in the canteen when it happened, and that because I was married to him once doesn't mean to say that I'm in any way connected with the crime.'

'When did you last see him, for any length of time?'

She tried to hide the fact that this particular question worried her, she shrugged her shoulders, pouted a bit, moved around, anything.

'Three, four months ago? We met occasionally at cocktail parties of course, but our relationship was severed the day we were divorced.'

'Really?' I said, not believing a word of it. 'Did April ever see him?'

The look she gave me wasn't a look at all, it was a death wish aimed at my head which worked its way downwards to my toes, but it confirmed my suspicions that little April was somehow involved in the whole affair and that old Mum-bird was doing a good bit of protecting.

'Look, Miss Danton, sooner or later you'll need the help of a man who knows the ins and outs of crime. I know enough about you and your daughter to sense that something is not quite as it should be, if you want me to help I will do so, but I must be put fully in the picture.'

I watched her as she poured herself a large tot of Scotch and, as an after-thought, poured one out for me too. She was chewing her lower lip which caused some of her lipstick to tinge her white teeth, but she still commanded my respect.

'When I asked you to confirm the rumour that my first husband, Oscar, was having an affair with Noelle Knowles, I wanted to know this to find out whether Justin cared.'

'Why?'

'Because if he didn't it meant that there was someone else in his life.'

She played around with the ice cube in her glass, tears could have been welling up in her eyes.

'Your teenage daughter?'

'I don't know. I just don't know.'

Right back there in my little old subconscious I had worked along the right hunch. It was fantastic how I did it. I had to admit that Zeelah had had to spell it out for me, but I was glad my unaided intuition had put me on the right tracks. With a bit more practice I might start making a profit, getting a reputation, opening up a bigger business.

'Are you taking your daughter with you?' I asked.

'Do you think she'd come? No. I just don't want to be around when all the dirt comes up. I've had enough bad publicity with my two divorces . . . and she won't want me.'

'Do you suspect her?' It was a sudden

question, I wanted to take her by surprise.

'Of what? The murder? No! The only thing she's guilty of is looking young and innocent.'

'And not being the latter?'

'Oh she's innocent enough. She doesn't know what sort of world she's in yet. I haven't been the best mother.'

I allowed myself three seconds to think of April, but the image was blurred. A young thing with long blonde hair and a cheeky smile, dimples perhaps. I could see her still sucking a lollipop.

'I'd like you to keep an eye on her Mr. Flute and let me know what she's up to. I'll pay you now.'

Unexpectedly she handed me a cheque which she had already written out.

'This should cover all your expenses and maybe some of hers should you have to force her to travel.'

The cheque was for two hundred guineas and I realized it carried plenty of responsibility.

'Just let me check on what you want me to do. You want me to look after April?'

'Yes. When you've found her.'

'You don't know where she is?'

'No idea. Her father may be taking care of her . . . which isn't the best thing for her.'

'Supposing she is with her father, what do I do?'

'Just let me know. I'll contact you at your office as soon as I know where I'm going.'

I took out my wallet, slipped the folded cheque in safely and tucked it back into my pocket. Crossing the room I stood a few feet back from the window and looked out at the calm sunbathed street. Opposite there was a terrace of houses identical to the one we were in, to the right two insignificant looking cars were parked on the same side of the road, to the left one insignificant-looking detective constable dressed up as a travelling salesman waiting to see who would go in, or come out of, Zeelah's front door.

6

I was confident that I hadn't been followed as far as Zeelah's house and I was sure the man hadn't been there when I entered the place. He hadn't been there long and all I had to do was make sure he didn't spot me leaving.

'Is there a way out the back?' I asked.

'No. The only other exit is by the basement steps, but they give out onto the street. Why?'

'There's a policeman watching the house out there.'

'That man? How do you know he's a policeman?'

'He's been studying that map long enough to know his way around blindfolded and seems particularly interested in this place. What else could he be?'

'A tourist, lost.'

'Lost indeed, the map he's looking at is one of North Wales. They really ought to pay more attention to detail.'

I moved away from the window and lost myself in a deep armchair.

'What do we do?' asked the anxious actress.

'You should leave as soon as possible, go to a hotel, contact the police from there, then make for the Continent.'

'What will you do?'

'I'll stay here till the coast is clear. He'll follow you, the moment he's gone, I'll go. How long will it take you to pack?'

'I'm ready to go. I packed as soon as I got back.'

'Then leave now. The Press boys will be here sooner than you think.'

'Could you ring for a cab? I'll get my coat.'

Nervous, Zeelah left the room and went upstairs. I dialled a taxi number, asked a deep voice for a cab to come round, and put down the receiver. From behind the curtains I watched the detective watching the house. He was bored and couldn't quite think what else to do after folding up the map, unfolding it and folding it again. He hadn't been ready to stand in quite such a deserted street and the whole operation of seeming casual was becoming difficult. I felt like going out and telling him that he could observe the whole of the street from the corner, where he himself would be less conspicuous — but it wasn't really up to me.

Zeelah came down with a small suitcase just as a taxi drew up at the door. I apologized for not being able to behave like a gentleman, but under the circumstances it would not be very cautious for me to see her to the cab.

We arranged that she would give me a ring as soon as she was settled, said goodbye briefly, and she pulled the door to behind her.

I didn't watch her getting into the taxi but instead studied the antics of the salesman-tourist who was now having a field day. While keeping an eye on Zeelah's movements he was still pretending to read his map, then the moment the cab drove away he moved off at speed.

I had to open the door wider to see where he was going. At the end of the street a car was waiting for him, the

Metropolitan police were using everything they had on hand.

I left the door slightly open and decided to have a peep upstairs to gauge how my client and her daughter lived before leaving the premises.

The house had four floors, basement, ground, first, and second. Zeelah Danton's room was on the first, a spacious square affair decorated in light blues and greens the walls hung with drapes on which hung a number of small valuable oil paintings. The effect was one of intense luxury. A door led off to a well furnished bathroom, still humid, still smelling heavily of powerful scent. I opened a few drawers but they didn't reveal anything unfamiliar. A good stock of stockings, a hundred and twenty silk scarves, bottles of various face conditioners, nail varnish, nail varnish removers, hair tints, lotions, dyes, eye shadows, green blue and purple, scissors, razors, a Pifco Vibrator, costume jewellery in abundance . . . a woman's realm.

As I stood up from the dressing table I glanced out of the window and down into the street and blinked — twice. A few yards down the road, still reading his map of North Wales was my friend the detective constable. The car had gone after Zeelah but not him. He was going to wait for April or anyone else that came along, and I was going to be kept prisoner until I thought up some brilliant idea. Whatever else I did I could not afford to be seen anywhere near Zeelah's house; I would have to think seriously of disguising myself somehow, or something.

I sighed a deep sigh and decided to go on with my investigation, maybe I would find a cellar full of gin which would help pass the time of day. I moved on, upwards.

Upstairs the layout was exactly the same but the decor was very different. April's room was masculine, or studentish anyway, without pin-ups, no Presleys, no Brandos, no Warren Beattys — just a fair-sized photograph of Dad, Oscar Lovaks himself in dinner jacket at a film première, and another one of Mum.

There was a desk, a low bed, the walls were dull green, the curtains chintz. For a film star she wasn't living it up any, not in her own room at least.

Her bathroom had no clues to offer either, a white tiled affair with a shower was the only luxury. I was disappointed and decided that maybe she hadn't been paid yet.

I sat down at her small school like desk and opened a few drawers. At sixteen I was sure she had some secret hidden somewhere waiting to be discovered. I was a detective and right on the spot to discover it. I found three indian rubbers, a box of unused crayons, two virgin pads of writing paper, an empty 1958 diary and a green elastic band in the top drawer.

Underneath was more interesting. A hardly used cheque book, a paying-in book with two entries, both under a hundred pounds, a ready reckoner and a slide rule. In the bottom drawer a black tin box with all her secrets presumably in it looked comfortably settled in one corner. It was locked, all I had to do was find the key.

The cupboard was crammed with

clothes, old clothes and new ones, they all had that unscented school girl smell that sends pimply schoolboys raving mad, but there was nothing to excite me.

Just for kicks I got down on all fours and looked under the bed and came up with an old piece of electric flex covered with dust and a very worn slipper. No key. When I got to my feet I found myself staring at a man staring at me.

He was short, young, not too well dressed, had a slightly dirty shirt, crooked bow tie and his hair was thick and black.

'Like, the door was open so I walked in,' he said. He was from somewhere in Fleet Street and was even proud of it. I should have closed the door and bolted it. These characters had no respect for other people's property at all!

'No deal here,' I said, opening another cupboard. 'Got a camera?'

'Downstairs.'

'This is the kid's bedroom.'

'Who's interested in the kid?'

'She's bigger news than Mum, isn't she?' I said.

'Not any more.'

'No? Why not?'

'Mum did it, they say.'

It hadn't taken long, a rumour had been started by someone and it was spreading like wildfire.

'Who told you?' I asked.

'My editor.'

'Who told him?'

'One of the boys. Who you from?'

'Freelance. I got an angle though, which'll be worth something.'

'Yeah? Split?'

'Got a car?'

'Sure.'

'Let's get out of here and I'll tell you on the way. This place will be hot with the Yard any minute.'

'Go on, a scoop?'

'Maybe. Zeelah Danton skipped it to the Continent!'

'Wow! Got any more to that story?'

'The lot.'

'Come on then, we'll catch the first edition. Whiz! Like this means promotion — if it ever existed. What's your name kiddo?'

We left the house in a hurry and

crammed into the mini car that the cameraman was driving. I didn't care too much that I was sitting up against the wrong end of the tripod, what was important was that no one should see me come out of the house.

The fact that I was no longer a prisoner in Zeelah's house was one step better, but I was now a prisoner of the Fleet Street boys. They thought I had hot news and somehow I had to get out of the car and away before they found out it was a lie. Suddenly I had an inspiration and talked about it.

'Like,' I said, anyone could be in Fleet Street. 'Like you wouldn't mind having a snap of who did it?'

'Mac, we would not.'

'I know where to go.'

'What? Why didn't you say so before?'

'I had other preoccupations Booboo. Turn left down here.'

The cameraman turned left. We were in the Strand and near enough the Savoy to spit at it. I asked them to stop, climbed out and reassured them by a wink that I'd be back with good news. I crossed the road and entered the hotel.

Only one thing was worrying me, the thought of Furrows waiting for me to call him up. It pained me to think of the poor man anxiously chewing his nails for the tinkle of the telephone bell. I had to put an end to his agony.

I found my way to a carpeted and curtained telephone booth, asked the clear delicious voice for a line and was told to give her the number I wanted. The hotel made a profit on telephone calls, to pay for the carpet and curtains.

'Nine, nine, nine,' I said.

'Ooh!' she said and put me through ever so quick.

'Fire, police or ambulance?' a stern lesbian voice asked.

'Scotland Yard please, Detective Inspector John Furrows.'

'You'll have to dial Whitehall 1212.'

'I haven't any money and I'm in a call box.'

'What is your name?'

'Adam Flute.'

'Hold the line.'

I got through by the time I had finished

a new cigarette, and examined the stubble on my chin in the small delicate gold mirror on the pink wall.

'Mr. Furrows? Flute here.'

'Yes Flute. Seen your client?'

'I've come to a decision.'

'Good. Are you going to tell me who your client is or will I have to waste a lot of time asking you unnecessary questions?'

'I'll tell you.'

'Fine, there's no time like the present, is there?'

'No,' I said, then, 'Justin Joyce.'

'Justin Joyce! He was your client?'

'Yes.'

'Why didn't you tell me before?'

'Pride I suppose. One doesn't like to admit losing a client one has been payed to protect.'

'You were protecting him? What from?'

'Well, I wasn't exactly protecting him, I was sort of investigating whether a few phone calls he had been receiving were legitimate.'

'When did he come to you?'

'Two days ago he rang up from Cannes

and asked me to go and see him down there.'

'And did you?'

'Yes. I thought I had the answer to his problem — his wife, Noelle Knowles — the big publicity stunt.'

'And do you think that was the answer?'

'Frankly, yes. I don't think the calls were in any way connected with the murder. If I were you I'd disregard them completely, in fact, I don't think I can really help you at all.'

'What sort of calls were they?'

He was being sticky, I hadn't thought too much about this concocted story and I had to be careful not to get too involved.

' ''We-think-you're-a-ham'' type calls, insults, you know.'

'What were you doing at the studios then?'

'He was there for rehearsals between flights and it was the only time I could see him . . . I didn't though. He was dead when I met him.'

'All right Flute, if you could come down when it's convenient and sign a statement about what you've just said, I'd be grateful.'

'Fine,' I said, disguising a sigh of relief.

'Oh, and by the way, where did he get these calls, in France?'

'No, in England, before he left.'

'Mmm,' he said as though he doubted me. 'You haven't by chance heard of a man called Dick Forsyth?'

The hair just behind my neck did a little dance and I twitched nervously for a second or two.

'Dick Forsyth? Why yes!'

'A friend of yours?'

'Shall we say an invention of mine. It was a name I used to get into the studio . . . I do that sometimes when I feel it's going to be difficult . . . a little lie to the receptionists, you know . . . a game . . . like?'

'We haven't the time to play games in the Force Mr. Flute. I will see you when you come to sign your statement.'

He rang off and left me alone with the dead receiver, alone except for the two Fleet Street boys who were standing and waiting for me outside the booth.

'She's gone,' I said, looking depressed.

'Yeah?'

'Yeah, back home. If you hurry you'll get a picture of her being arrested.'

They couldn't afford to waste time checking on the story, I had learnt that much. I watched them skip out of the hotel, followed them at a safe distance and got into a taxi. I gave the driver my address, sat well back in the seat and chewed over the facts and the end of my thumb.

I didn't think I'd said anything too rash to Furrows, the lie about me protecting Joyce was woolly enough not to bother him. I would have to avoid signing a statement for a while till I had made contact with April and asked her a few questions. If the girl was in trouble I would have to see that she didn't make things worse for herself.

Glancing out of the window I noticed the newspaper boards and the big headlines. They were bold, brief and forced the passers-by to purchase.

'FILM STAR MURDERED — JUSTIN JOYCE
STABBED TO DEATH'
'B.B.C. MURDER — ACTOR MASSACRED'

I stopped the cab at the next corner, got out and bought one of the evening papers that promised the best story of all.

'BLOOD BATH AT TV STUDIOS. FILM STAR DECAPITATED'

In the back of the cab I glanced at the front page account of what happened. It was the best fiction I had read for some time and even the guess work hadn't been written on the spot. The story, however, prepared the readers for a really juicy breakfast treat the following morning. No one, it was obvious, knew anything.

'That film star copped it,' the driver said with a smirk as I paid my fare. He had never been handsome enough to contemplate a film career and was pleased that those who had sometimes came to a sticky end.

'Yes,' I said. 'Wonder who did it?'

'Gawd knows. They've got all my sympathy anyway.'

I walked into the block of flats, pressed the lift button and waited for the cage to come down.

The middle page spread of the evening paper had gone to town on Justin's life. Zeelah was featured, so was Noelle Knowles and so was April. The article was cleverly written and hinted that any one of them might have done it, what the reporter obviously didn't know was that Justin had been killed with a heavy broadsword, a weapon which only a strong man could have used, certainly not a woman.

Looking forward to a cup of hot black coffee and a nice sit down, I climbed into the lift and pressed the top floor button.

On the top floor, just seven inches the other side of the lift gates, I found a girl standing, smiling at me. She was five foot four inches tall, had raven black hair down to her shoulders, a slightly oriental look about her face, almond shaped eyes, white-pink lips and a figure that was made to excite any studio technician. I had seen her before and her name was Pascale Anjoux.

7

I opened the door of my flat for her and showed her in. She was wearing a threequarter black leather coat, tight white twill trousers and a heavy knit tan roller neck sweater, but the clothes didn't hide her shape.

She walked straight to the window and onto the balcony and looked across the park.

'What a wonderful view!'

I followed her onto the balcony and stood just behind her. Since she was born her mother had bathed her in scent and she couldn't wink without sending a transparent cloud of this heavy sexy aroma a quarter of a mile all round her.

'At night it's even better, when there's a moon that is. The London sky's a deep purple and the lights below make it kind of fairytale like,' I said, breathing in.

'I'd like to see it at night,' she said with enthusiasm.

We were off to a good start.

'What can I do for you Miss . . . Mrs . . . ?'

'Oh. My name is Pascale Anjoux,' she said simply. Her French accent was more obvious when she pronounced her name.

'It sounds familiar.'

'I am an actress on the films, but not very famous, yet.'

'Of course!' I said, still breathing.

I couldn't believe it was coincidence that had brought her here, but the way she had looked at me gave me the impression she hadn't seen me before. It was a surprised look as though she had expected someone older, or maybe less handsome.

'I . . . I find it difficult . . . it is difficult for me to start,' she said turning and looking innocent.

'Let me make it easier for you. Let's sit down and just have a chat about the weather first. How did you come to hear about me?'

I guided her back into the living room and we sat down opposite each other in the ample blue armchairs. She was wearing soft flat black shoes and silk stockings under her trousers. On the little finger of her left hand she wore a solitaire which just meant that at one time she had known someone with money, or still did. I guessed she was about eighteen.

'I looked you up in the classified directory,' she said, answering my question.

'I see. Why did you choose me, there are other agencies?'

'I liked the sound of your name, not too serious. And you were nearest to the studios.'

'The studios?' I could look very dumb sometimes.

'The BBC Television studios, they are at Shepherd's Bush.'

She was settling in nicely now and looking around the room to see how I lived. I lived well.

'Are you in trouble?'

'Not yet.'

'Perhaps you're connected with this murder at the studios?' I said, as though I thought I was being pretty clever.

'You've heard about it?'

'I read the evening papers.'

'Then I do not have to explain myself too much.'

'The more you do the better for me,' I said.

'Well,' she started, hesitated, then smiled shyly, 'it sounds silly, but I'm frightened.'

'Of what?'

'Of the murderer.'

'You know who it is?'

'I think so.'

'And you're frightened that you might be attacked because you know too much?'

'Yes.'

Either she was genuine and needed help or she was putting on an act to get someone's sympathy. Those were two possibilities there was a third, she could be trying to find out how involved I was in the whole affair. Whatever her reasons were for hunting me out, I couldn't lose if she told me who the criminal was.

'Who did it?' I asked.

'Will you help me?'

'Yes, if I can.'

'Then I would like you to accompany me to my apartment.'

110

It was an attractive proposition but somewhere there was a catch in it.

'And you'll tell me who killed Justin when we get there?'

'Yes.'

I didn't just look at her, I looked through her as though I knew exactly what she was up to. I had a pretty good idea. She wasn't working for herself, that was clear, but whoever she was working for had some sort of hold on her.

'What about money?' I said, bluntly.

'Oh, I'll pay you.'

'Have you got a car?'

'Yes, it's outside.'

'How far is it to your flat?'

'Not far, the other side of London.'

On the way something would happen, I'd get sapped, or pushed out of the window or doped again, the whole idea reeked of deceit. She was standing up now because I had stood up and we were ambling towards the door.

'Why don't you want to talk here?' I asked.

'I . . . there's something I want to show you.'

'Etchings?' I suggested.

She smiled, laughed nearly, relieved that I wasn't making things too difficult for her. She was as worried about being hunted by a killer as I was about not knowing how to spend money. I had my hand on the door now and was about to open it, but I delayed a bit and looked at her more seriously.

'What if someone's waiting for you downstairs?'

'Who?'

'The person who's going to kill you.'

Suddenly she looked frightened, as frightened as any bad actress when she's about to be killed for the third retake.

'I hadn't thought of that.'

'Well don't worry, I'll protect you.'

My smile warned her that I wasn't taking her problem too seriously. I moved from the door and started towards the bedroom.

'What are you doing?'

'Getting a revolver, what else? I don't like meeting potential killers unarmed.' She was still worried by my smile, so I added, 'While you're waiting you might like to make a phone call — to tell them that I've agreed to come with you.'

She looked perplexed. There was fear in her eyes, the fear girls of eighteen have of being made to look a fool. She recovered quickly.

'I'm sorry I don't understand you.'

'You haven't the slightest idea who killed Justin Joyce, have you?'

I was standing in the bedroom doorway and she could easily open the front door and leave the flat, but to stop her I started taking my jacket off. It was a simple little move, there was no explanation why I was doing it and her curiosity made her stay to find out.

'Have you?' I repeated in a loud voice.

She didn't answer but just looked at me startled, when I looked angry I was even more handsome.

'Someone in your life is so powerful they've managed to make you come here and do some very dirty work, haven't they?'

She still didn't say anything. I was searching the pockets of my jacket now, for nothing, but she didn't know that and was even more curious.

'I know who it is Miss Anjoux, I know who you're working for and why they want me wherever it is that you're supposed to take me.'

She didn't know what to say, or do. I had taken my cufflinks off and I had started taking my tie off as well. The whole act impressed me if no one else. She really looked rather lovely, perplexed as she was and a trifle frightened.

'Did you know, Miss Anjoux, that I was working for Justin. Did you know that he and I were the greatest of buddies and that he told me everything that went on in his life?'

This, for a reason I hadn't even suspected, made her blush. She looked down at her shoes then up again and tried to take a step forward, but she had nowhere in particular to go.

I let my jacket and tie drop to the floor and stared at her coldly. The girl had a guilt complex and knew plenty that I wanted to know, by fair means or foul I was going to find out everything.

'Do you know where April Mundy is

now?' I asked, sharply.

'No.'

'Well I do.'

'You do? Where?'

This interested her. This really interested her, her tongue was hanging out she
was so thirsty for the answer.

'I'll tell you where April is if you tell me
what you came for. The real reason.'

I badly needed a cigarette so I turned
round and looked around the bedroom
for one which might have been left in a
packet. I hadn't made the bed and as it
was the daily's day off she hadn't made it
either. The room was pretty untidy and
with the sheets exposed and my pyjamas
bundled in one corner, a couple of socks
making love on the carpet and three
discarded shirts hanging their heads over
the back of a chair it wasn't the place one
invited visitors to see. But she came in all
the same.

I was searching the small drawer of my
night table when I sensed her a few feet
behind me. I turned and gave her one of
those surprised looks one gives people
when they're taking off their sweaters and

they've already taken off their black leather coats.

I didn't say anything but just watched her. She knew she had me spellbound, her thin brown arms and the quarter inch of silk strap which held up her tiny bra were enough to hold anyone spellbound. I opened my mouth to breathe better and try to tell myself that here was danger heading for me at a terrible speed.

She was close enough now for me to get the full impact of her perfume again. Under the sweater she only wore this small white bra, and under that . . . I knew exactly what there was.

I pulled myself together a little and looked down at her. She was examining my face for some sort of expression which would tell her she had me where she wanted me, I just didn't know whether she was right or not.

'The door's not closed,' I tried, failing to break the spell.

'Does it matter?'

Her fine delicate hands were pressing themselves flat against my white shirt and she was looking at me with deep devotion.

'I want you,' she whispered standing on tiptoe and opening her lips just a fraction, 'Badly.'

I had been wanted badly by a few feverish women in my time but never quite so blatantly, if she hadn't said a word and kept her distance, or flirted for a few hours beforehand as a warm up, I might have been had, but this was overdoing it.

Taking hold of her small wrists I very gently pushed her away, then had another thought. Still holding her I turned her round, backed her towards the open bed and pushed her onto it. The whole scene was due for a Certificate X any minute.

Wrestling her wrist from my grip, she gently put her arm round my neck and pulled me towards her. This was the moment I thought.

'Darling,' I said.

'Yes?' Her eyes were all loving, all wondering, all in awe at the beauty of the world.

'Darling,' I repeated for effect. 'Do you

really think that I am as vulnerable as I look — that I don't know what you're up to?'

'Mmmm?' Her forehead frowned. Things weren't going quite right.

'Throwing yourself at me in this way isn't going to get you anywhere. If you think you're going to play hard to get just when my temperature is at boiling point so that you can make me promise anything you want — you're wrong. I'm not going to let my temperature rise at all.'

So saying I pulled away unexpectedly and waited for the inevitable frenzied scene to follow. Tears maybe, a slam across the face, a fit of uncontrollable rage? But she didn't move. For about ten long seconds she looked at me, then started laughing.

'Joke?' I said.

'You are so serious Mr. Flute! So intense, you should relax a bit more.'

I smiled. It was hard, but I smiled and made it look genuine. She had tried something, it hadn't worked, but it didn't bother her too much.

I picked up my tie from the floor, put it on, tied it, hitched up my trousers and started for the living room with an idea in mind about a drink.

'You wouldn't like to tell me what it is you really want?' I asked over my shoulder.

'You! To come with me, to meet a friend.'

'No friend would ever have asked you to do what you just did. It was very dangerous.'

'Pooh! I can look after myself.'

It was the arrogant way in which she said it that prompted me to give her the scare of her life. Spinning round on my heels I grabbed hold of her arm and pulled her towards me. She was so small and so light that hugging her was tantamount to crushing her — but it didn't stop me. The more she resisted the more I tightened my grip, till finally she gave in and let herself go limp.

I lifted her clean off the ground and like an inflamed lover carried her back to the bed. That was when she gave her first genuine scream, the second was when I changed my mind and took her to the bathroom to drop her unceremoniously in the bath and turned on the shower.

When I turned it off to stop her shrieking I heard the telephone ring. I left her to get out of the tub alone and crossed the bedroom to pick up the receiver. It was Furrows.

I listened calmly to what he had to say, agreed to keep in contact and my eyes and ears open, then replaced the receiver.

When Pascale, wet and sexy, appeared in the bathroom doorway I didn't smile back at her childish grin.

'They've made an arrest,' was all I said.

8

When little girls get scolded they either go off and sulk for a few days or pull themselves together and put on a big intelligent act. Pascale did the latter, she sat right down on the sofa, after taking off her damp bra and trousers and putting on my dressing gown, lit herself a cigarette and tried to work out what impression she had made on me.

I was by the sideboard fixing both of us a drink and also trying to figure things out. The arrest story was just an inspiration I had thrown at her to draw her out. All Furrows had told me was that he would be at his divisional headquarters until midnight if I wanted to come over and make that statement.

On the Pascale Anjoux angle I was going to let my old hunches fling themselves around a bit. She was someone's stooge and I wanted to find out whose.

'Tell me about yourself,' I started, I was genuinely interested and liked listening to that quaint French accent. 'What's your background?'

'Oh, my parents are very rich, my father is in the Chambre des Deputes.'

'Are you the only child?'

'Yes.'

'Spoilt.'

'Am I spoilt?'

'Maybe not, maybe you're just immature — you must be to have acted like you did.'

It worked like a dream. She started getting annoyed but was sensible enough to check herself.

'I did it purely to help someone out.'

It didn't sound convincing and I didn't look convinced. She was sitting forward with her elbows hard down on her knees, she was clutching her glass and seemed worried.

'Supposing you tell me what it's all about, then maybe I can really help.'

'I think I have been stupid. I think I have been very stupid.' She wasn't talking to me but to the glass. It was half full and it had room to take any self criticism from any drinker.

'You know Oscar Lovaks?' she asked, after a while.

'Yes, thank you.'

'I did it for him.'

I blinked. I was surprised, even shocked, that a man could have so much power over people.

'Did he ask you to fling yourself at me?'

'No, just to get you — by any means.'

'He wants to see me?'

'Yes.'

'What for?'

'I don't know. I just do as I'm told.'

'You too? Has he got you under contract or something?'

'No. If he had I wouldn't act this way, it's because he hasn't — but he's promised to.'

'Does he treat all his stars like dirt?'

'Stars? I'm not a star. I know exactly what I'm worth to a film producer — nothing! Until I make a good film. Oscar makes good films.'

I uncrossed and recrossed my legs. I was feeling really nervous. This was a character I hadn't met before, a big business man in a big business who was playing out his life like one of his film scripts.

'You'll be telling me next he had Justin killed.'

'No. Oscar would not have Justin killed, he would do it himself.'

'That strikes him off the suspect list then.'

'Why?'

'Unless he used a long range missile it's unlikely he killed Justin.'

'But he was at the studios.'

'When?'

'When it happened.'

I gulped down my dry martini and listened to my heart beating. Where had I been all day? What was I doing here listening to a teenager telling me everything I ought to know?

'Are you sure?'

'Of course I'm sure, he and Noelle Knowles were recording an interview for the news. He's managed to pull off a fantastic stunt.'

With no ulterior motives I got up and

sat down right next to her on the sofa.

'Just start right at the beginning will you, tell me everything you know, then I promise I'll accompany you to wherever it is you want me to go.'

'Justin Joyce, Noelle Knowles and April Mundy are cast in a film called *Lonely are the Damned* which Oscar Lovaks is making at Elstree.'

'Yes,' I said.

'But all three of them were on location in the South of France until yesterday.'

'Were they?' I said. 'April as well?'

'April as well. She came back with Justin for the rehearsal of this Television Play that I'm also in, and Oscar and Noelle came back ... to get some publicity.'

'I see,' I said, seeing, or nearly.

'He also came back for the play of course,' she added.

'Who Oscar?'

'Yes.'

'Why of course? He's nothing to do with the production is he?'

'Not much, he only wrote the damn thing.'

I got up to help myself to another drink. The film and television world was complicated enough, but for one madman to be running the whole business was really getting me mixed up.

'He was supervising the rehearsal, I suppose?'

'And keeping an eye on his valuable actors. I think he really came this time to appease Noelle.'

'Why did she need appeasing?'

'Me. I'm going to be in the big picture, taking a fair sized part, and I'm in the play taking a fair sized part. She's in the picture taking not such a big part and she's not in the play at all. Instead there's Lovaks's first wife — Zeelah — and his daughter!'

'What is Noelle to Lovaks that he bothers about her?'

Pascale shrugged her shoulders, the whole subject seemed to be distasteful to her.

'What is Noelle to anyone? She charmed Justin out of Zeelah's arms, and Zeelah had money, then she charmed Lovaks into giving her a part.'

'What was all this suicide set-up for then?'

'It wasn't a set-up at first. When she felt she wasn't going to get what she wanted she said she would do herself in. So Oscar told her to go right ahead. I was there when he told her — on the telephone. He knew she wouldn't do anything, but phoned the publicity boys all the same, and they sprang the story before the deed was done.'

'All this doesn't explain why Lovaks should ask you to come here and put on the act that you did.'

'He wants to see you. Thinks you could help him.'

'Why didn't he just ring me up? Or come and see me himself.'

'Oscar? Come and see you? He's a film tycoon.'

I didn't feel insulted or anything but I did just wonder why a tycoon couldn't come and see me, or at least give me a ring. Maybe I didn't understand tycoons or something.

'Oscar has such power that everybody moves everything out of the way for him.

Like I'm doing. Oscar said to me, 'Bring me Flute' and I will . . . won't I?'

I didn't commit myself but just looked at her. She was cute in my dressing gown, the silk stuck to her back and legs and made her figure appealing.

'You don't know these people,' she said, after draining her glass. 'The police don't know them. They don't live on this earth at all. They move at the speed of lightning. If Oscar decides to have lunch in New York tomorrow he'll have lunch in New York tomorrow and he'll decide an hour before the plane leaves for New York. He's God! At least he thinks he is.'

So on me accepting or refusing to accompany her depended her film career. That's what it all added up to. 'Get Flute' those were her orders, if she carried them out successfully he would be pleased with her, and that was all she wanted.

It was one of those occasions when I could have probably named my price. She would have found the money somehow, but I was too proud, or too honest, or I liked her shape in my dressing gown. Besides, I felt it would do me good to meet Lovaks again.

Her bra and trousers were dry enough now for her to slip them on. She spent a few minutes looking at herself in the mirror, then sighed a deep sigh.

'You haven't any lipstick, by chance?' she asked. 'I look terrible.'

'In the left-hand drawer of the dressing table.'

She was surprised, astounded, she opened the drawer and looked at the assortment of beauty aids that were there.

'Are you married?'

'No.'

'You have a mistress?'

'No.'

'Why all this? Surely . . . '

'No, not that either. I just keep a stock for emergencies such as this. A lot of women cry when they come here, and I don't like them leaving the premises looking sad. It's bad for business.'

'Why do they cry?' She was combing back her black hair and I was just behind her breathing in deeply.

'All sorts of reasons. A Private Detective is usually employed by unhappy people who have lost something.'

'Like a dog you mean?' She was using a bright orange lipstick now which didn't suit her.

'Or a husband,' I said.

She didn't fancy the orange either, tried the other three shades available and in the end wiped them all off.

'Shall we go?'

'I'm ready,' I said.

★ ★ ★

Downstairs, parked behind my car, was a long, white, red upholstered, drop head, chauffeur driven Cadillac which looked more like a luxury launch than a luxury launch. The chauffeur was a studio employee with a union card, so he didn't get out of his seat to open the door for Miss Anjoux but gave her a look that didn't carry much respect. Maybe she had made the mistake of sitting in the front seat with him on the way to my flat or perhaps he was hoping to be a film star himself.

The drive through London's West End

in the middle of the rush hour was amusing, if nothing else. It certainly wasn't very warm.

The people standing in the bus queues looked at us as though we were people who thought they should be recognized. Pascale waved once or twice at imaginary fans and I just wondered how people managed to stand in bus queues day in day out come rain or shine. I felt sorry for them, but didn't offer any of them a lift. It wasn't my car.

We oozed across Westminster Bridge between two buses, turned left and eventually buried ourselves deep in Dockland. I had never liked Dockland much when alone in the dark, but in broad daylight with a sexy brunette next to me in a car which spelt loot with a capital 'L' I felt even more insecure. One big lorry, a couple of beefy dockers and that would be it. But the journey was as uneventful as the empty streets and we came to an unexpected halt outside a disused warehouse.

The chauffeur man leaned back and lit a cigarette, watching Pascale and I in his driving mirror as we climbed out. This was apparently our destination.

Worried, I followed the Anjoux girl down a dark passage, which had black damp walls, and felt a little happier at the sight of a civilised brass lantern hanging from the low rafters outside a white painted door.

The light wasn't on so I couldn't see, but Pascale knew where the bell was and used it. A few seconds later the door opened and a butler of sorts opened the door. He had black trousers and a white top coat, but I reckoned he only opened doors to people in the evenings. Both his hands were tatooed down to the fingers and on his left cheek he had a very unpleasant scar. Maybe he was just a stunt man.

I followed Pascale up the very steep and narrow red carpeted stairs and glanced at the prints hung on the walls. They were carefully chosen racing prints and spelt luxury.

At the top of the stairs we turned sharp left and I found myself in a studio the size of Wembley Stadium, carpeted all white with very few but well chosen pieces of furniture and a bay window which had a panoramic view of Tower Bridge, the dome of St Paul's and the river. Lovaks couldn't have done less.

He was sitting, hunched up on the edge of a vast divan and in front of him was an equally vast television set.

Without looking up or around, he signalled us to sit down and keep quiet, so with a nervous Pascale I sat down on a smaller divan within eyeshot of the light blue screen.

The programme that was catching Lovaks' attention was a special feature, and a chubby faced gentleman with glasses was working up to a dramatic story about Hollywood and film stars.

'If you heard the news just before this programme or read this evening's papers,' he said with his sincere serious face, 'you will have heard about the quite incredible death of Justin Joyce, the film star. Shortly before his body was found, we actually interviewed his wife, star of stage and screen Miss Noelle Knowles, who only yesterday was herself involved in a dramatic situation with her producer, Oscar Lovaks.'

There followed the usual panning in and panning out, dissolving and fading in routine, we got a close-up of an even chubbier gentleman and then a close-up of Noelle.

The interview was enlightening. It was a talk by Lovaks to the interviewer about how Noelle had failed to kill herself. She managed to say four words, three of which were 'yes'. The story of the suicide, he said, had been completely fabricated from the start by himself not to get publicity for his new film — *Lonely are the Damned* — but to get Miss Knowles into the right mood for a scene in the film when she attempts to take her own life.

I was sitting two feet away from the man who had invented all these lies and was astonished by the nerve he had had and the success with which he had managed to get national coverage. It was because he didn't care a damn about anyone that he was sitting there in a luxury apartment with heaven knows how many other luxury apartments dotted around the globe with, presumably, any number of beautiful women ready to slave for him. I admired him, nearly as much as he admired himself.

When the close-up of his badly shaven chin and the interviewer's caustic comments had faded, to be replaced by a couple of jeaned up guitarists, Lovaks leaned back, pressed a button on a small control gadget he held in his hand and the screen went blank.

'What did you think Pascale, did Noelle look good?'

'Not bad, she wasn't very favourably positioned though.'

'Not favourably positioned! You're joking! She wasn't positioned at all — and the way she crossed her legs. She'd better get to know herself better soon or we'll have to start hunting for talent again.'

He still hadn't looked round but from somewhere had produced a bowl of nuts and was cracking these between the palms of his hands.

'The whole thing was ruined by me anyway. I talk too much. I always talk too much. These young interviewers don't know their jobs, he should have interrupted me before I started. Hallo Flute, glad you decided to come.'

He was unravelling a stick of chewing gum now and inserting it into his mouth together with the nuts. He still hadn't looked round and I didn't know how he knew it was me. Maybe he didn't.

'Want you to do something for me, Flute,' he continued, studying more nuts, for fleas. 'I want you to find my daughter. I know you're already looking for her for my ex-wife . . . but I'll pay more if you get her to me first.'

I didn't say anything. He hadn't told me enough about the whole set-up for me to commit myself.

'My daughter, April Mundy — the name's my idea — is in this film I'm making and I need her for location shots, only the police want her as well. I'd like you to find her before they do.'

I glanced at Pascale who wasn't listening to the conversation. She was relaxed and happy. She had done her part of the bargain, all he had to do was sign her into this film.

'A question of time and money,' Lovaks continued. 'If they take her away for questioning it'll mean a delay on the shooting and she's already delayed us one day by disappearing. Another thing, she may have seen the crime and be in danger.'

'Any idea where she might be now?' I asked. I was interested.

'No. If I did I wouldn't be hiring you, and it's no use asking any of her friends I've tried them already.'

Like a big bear he got up off the divan and ambled across the room to the panoramic bay window. He looked like a scene from one of his films about film tycoons looking out of panoramic bay windows.

'You'll be getting acquainted with your part, Pascale, I hope. It's bigger than I had intended mainly due to Justin walking out on us like that. We haven't got much of him in the can, what we have we'll use because it'll sell the film, but you'll have to compete with Noelle and fall in love with some other guy. I'd better ring up New York and see who they can suggest.'

'You're changing the whole plot then?'

'Sure I'm changing the whole plot. Worried?'

'No.'

'Glad to hear it. Now you go back to your hotel and pack and drop Mr. Flute at his apartment on the way so that he can get down to work.'

Flute, the new employee got up and wondered whether he should bow. Pascale was feeling pretty high spirited and I felt a good time was going to be had by all except me and Justin Joyce whose body was now probably in the morgue being examined for foreign finger marks, bugs and other things.

I didn't enjoy the drive back to the flat much because I was working out just where I was going to start the hunt. I had to admit that I had put off getting down to work, but now I was engaged by Lovaks I presumed I could charge some pretty high expenses and somehow this stimulated me. I was a new man, a keen man, a man who would solve his client's problems very fast.

'You look unhappy,' my dark hostess said moving closer to me in the back of the vast car, because it was cold.

'I am.'

'Why?'

'Where do I start. Where does one find a blonde teenage girl who's running away from everyone?'

'You could start asking her friends.'

'Lovaks said he'd done that.'

'Then try her enemies.'

'Like who?'

'Like me.'

We were speeding up through the Park now and the wind was catching her hair and blowing it across her face. We were close enough for me to catch a few strands of it in my mouth if I wanted to, but I wasn't hungry.

'Where would you say April Munday was?' I asked.

'Maybe at the Villa Avril?'

'Where?'

'The Villa Avril, Regnes sur Mer, it's a lovely old house, a few miles from Nice. April bought it with what she earned from her last film, a sort of investment.'

'What makes you think she's there?'

'She told me it was the one place she'd go to if she ever wanted to get away from it all.'

'Did you mention this to Lovaks?'

'Yes.'

'What did he say?'

'Too obvious a place to go to. Everyone would start by looking for her there.'

'Would they?'

I was pensive. I had deep thoughts about the subject, but Pascale had lost interest in it. Something had taken her mind off it, maybe my fingers which were tickling her left ear lobe.

9

The Cadillac pulled up outside my block of flats and the hall porter was sufficiently impressed to open the door for me. Just to show him that I was really doing well I gave Pascale a big kiss, the kind a tired lover gives his tired loved one.

'Hope to see you again soon,' I said, meaning it.

'Maybe on the Cote d'Azur. I have rented an apartment in Cannes.'

Getting out of the car I noticed a young man was cleaning a Post Office van, he seemed more interested in me than in Pascale, which was worrying. On my way up to the flat I tried to organize my immediate future, I knew that if I wanted to find April I would have to chase up every lead, which meant I had to clear myself with the Yard and play ball with Furrows if I wanted to leave the country without difficulty.

Once in the flat I quickly collected a

few things together, a lightweight suit, a toothbrush, a passport, a few foreign currency notes from the emergency safe, then hopped out onto the balcony to look at the man who was still cleaning the Post Office van. It was spotless and so was his duster.

Downstairs in the hall I told the porter I might not be back for some time and out in the street I walked briskly up to the van cleaner and patted him gently on the shoulder.

'You can take me to Furrows now Mac. Save me the taxi fare and I'll save your face, won't say a word to anyone.'

★ ★ ★

Furrows was probably the busiest man in London. He had three people reading newspaper articles out to him, was answering two telephones and trying to think at the same time. He asked me to sit down and handed me a sheet of paper on which someone had very kindly typed out a very garbled version of what I'd told him on the phone.

A uniformed sergeant handed me a pen and I just waited till both receivers were in their cradles before I handed back the statement to Furrows — unsigned.

'My life is rather complicated right now Flute, I'm ready to have your licence withdrawn till this is over if you won't cooperate.'

'May I say a few words?'

'A few.'

'Does Miss Pascale Anjoux play any part in your jigsaw?'

'Why?'

'I've just spent the last two hours with her.'

'So?'

'She told me where April Mundy is hiding.'

Furrows waved his hand, indicated the door to everyone in the room and after three seconds of minor chaos the door closed and we were left alone.

'As briefly as possible, please.'

As briefly as I could I told him about Pascale's visit, about my meeting with Lovaks, about the missing April. I told him I could probably find the girl for him without raising any suspicions, if he let me go, and that it would save him a man or two and money.

'What makes you think I want Miss Mundy so badly?'

'She saw the crime didn't she?'

'You only have Lovaks's word for it — and that doesn't add up to much. You don't by chance suspect her do you?'

'No. How could a teenage girl kill a man taller than herself with a heavy broadsword?'

If I had suspected April I would not have taken on the job, or at least I would have attempted to keep her from the police till I knew more.

Furrows looked at me kindly, a smile whispered across his lips, he had something over me that I would hate hearing.

'I forgot to put you completely in the picture. Justin Joyce didn't die from a stabbing. He was shot. A .22 bullet was found where the sword was supposed to have gone in. This was the sword.'

From a drawer he produced Exhibit No. 1. A sawn-off broadsword made of light aluminium, a fake, a studio prop. It was the sort of dramatic touch that a girl like April might well think up. I wondered just what I had let myself in for.

'What would be her motive?' I asked.

'I didn't say I suspected her.'

'But if you did suspect her, what could be her motive?'

'I can think of quite a few. Justin Joyce was her stepfather, he made her mother unhappy by remarrying, he might have made her unhappy . . . he might have been rude about her father . . . She'll throw some light on the subject, when you find her.'

'You're letting me go then?'

'I can't stop you, can I?'

* * *

As soon as I got out of the plane at Nice Airport and crossed the tarmac in the burning sun I started thinking of how I could get out of the whole affair. The sky was too blue, the scent in the air too pleasant to even think of doing any work. Then I saw a couple of Continental Bentleys, a Mercedes or two and remembered how poor I was. I grabbed a taxi and told him to find me a cheap hotel.

After a wash and brush up, I opened the shutters which had cut me off from the view of the Square and looked down at the uncrowded streets of Regnes. The place was more than a village but less than a town. It was growing.

I took myself down the stairs to the small reception desk and asked the anaemic looking girl in black where I could find Miss Mundy's residence. She looked at me as though I were a tourist and gave me a vague route.

I walked up a steep hill, slowly, enjoying the warmth and the sight of the flowers and the new smells, then stopped outside a pair of high black gates. Behind the gates a tall house sporting white flaking walls rose three storeys high and about halfway up some drunken artist with a shaky hand had written the name 'VILLA AVRIL'.

With certain effort I pushed open one of the black gates; because it had swollen with the heat or the hinges were rusty it didn't open fully, I therefore had to squeeze myself through a small gap, but the effort was worth it.

I found myself in a courtyard which gave onto a terraced garden. The yard had at one time been tarmacked with red asphalt but the weather had not been good to it and the previous owners had not had it rolled, it was lumpy and cracked and weeds grew out of the various splits that looked like the aftermath of a minor earthquake.

To the left the tall house blocked the sky line and cast a big clear-cut black shadow across the garden and competed with two huge palm trees that were dusty with age and probably sheltered swarms of tarantulas under the massive expanse of their dull green moth eaten leaves.

I walked slowly past the high shuttered french windows which gave onto the terrace, round the side to what had once been a magnificent entrance. A heavy wrought iron gate with intertwining plants growing all over it led straight into a covered area. To the right an unexpected marble staircase rose straight up and seemed to serve all three floors of the house.

The marble had mastered time, here and there were a few cracks and there was nothing special that would have surprised an archaeologist, but the eye was caught by the grey-green arm and torso of a statue which had once stood on the empty pedestal at the top of the staircase.

I didn't go up but instead walked through the open pair of double doors which led into a barely furnished room. It smelt of fruit and stale french cigarettes, the walls were hung with a number of pre-Raphaelite paintings, on the floor there was a Persian rug covering a small part of the red tiled floor and, on it, an antique table inlaid with mosaic designs.

On either side of the table was an armchair upholstered in turquoise velvet which went as badly with everything as everything else and lying face down on an Egyptian styled gilt bedlike sofa was a medium sized blonde teenager.

I looked at her for a long time before I realized that she wasn't moving and didn't seem to be breathing.

A slight feeling of nausea started moving about in my stomach as I stepped forward to have a closer look.

April Mundy, neé April Lovaks, owner of the Villa Avril, star of large and small screen was — dead.

*　*　*

It was a familiar situation. Me alone in a room with a murder victim whom I was not meant to notice till I had left fingerprints everywhere. The same ingenious mind that had given me the appointment with Justin Joyce in the studio had concocted this one up.

It reeked of Lovaks and I looked around very carefully before making another move.

For the first time I noticed the tray on the table with the clean glasses and the jug full of water, the two bottles of whisky and gin, the silver cigarette box temptingly left shut and a silver table lighter all ready to take the prints of my innocent fingers.

I stayed still for quite a while thinking

things out carefully. My mind raced back to how I had come to be in this position, Pascale and her innocent manner, the way she had given me details of April's address. I wasn't fighting one man, I was up against an organization.

Luckily I hadn't left any trace of my existence in the empty house so far. I had nearly been caught, but had sensed the hook just in time to give me a chance to get out of it unscathed.

The more I thought of it the more I realized I had been an idiot to trust Pascale. After all she had honestly told me about herself and her ambitions, I should have been more careful of Lovaks's Zvengali powers. All his women were going to converge on me, all pointing their sharp nailed fingers at me and accusing me of Justin's and April's murders. In France I wouldn't stand a chance. I'd be locked up without a hope of proving my innocence and the police in England would laugh gently to themselves and put the Justin Joyce File in their pending tray.

But I was still free. To arrest me they

would have to have some sort of proof, and the fact that I was standing in a room with a dead girl wasn't much to go on. However I decided to move, and fast.

It was obviously unwise to go out the way I had come in, so I crossed the room and headed for the door on the other side of April's death bed. I was trying the handle and finding the locked door difficult to open when I froze. A distinct movement behind me told me I was no longer alone, and a voice confirmed it.

'What are you doing?'

Slowly I turned, looked down a little and pretended I wasn't surprised. She was alive and kneeling on the chaise longue with her yoke neck baby doll pyjamas showing me that though young she had enough maturity to know what it was all about. I blinked, smiled and tried to think of an answer.

'It's you!' she said after having a second look at me, sleep was still in her eyes. 'Mummy isn't here you know. She doesn't even know that I am.'

'Oh!' I said, and tried to look disappointed. 'Are you expecting anyone?'

'No. I'm all alone, why?'

'Who does know you're here?'

'I didn't think anyone did.'

I could feel a few beads of sweat running down my forehead. I wasn't hot physically, but mentally I didn't know what I was up to.

'Do you know who killed Justin?' I asked.

She gasped. A look of horror came into her eyes, quickly she got off the chaise longue and started backing away from me.

'Look — I've come here to help you!' I said.

She recovered pretty quickly, turned and leaned on the mosaic table. After a moment she helped herself to a generous glass of Perrier water.

Her dark silk brown limbs moved with the careless abandon of a young foal and from where I was standing it was difficult to know whether she was wearing anything under the bell top of her pyjamas.

'I'm a Private Detective, Miss Mundy, and someone's paid me a high salary to keep an eye on you, because they think you're in danger.'

'Who, Mummy?'

'I promised not to tell.'

'I thought you were one of Mum's . . . '

'I know what you thought.'

'I suppose it's father. Just the sort of idiotic thing he would think up. Big drama! Big story! Did *he* tell you that I knew who killed Justin?'

'He didn't tell me anything.'

'Well I don't. But if he's been saying that I do, then I probably am in danger.'

At this precise moment, we both heard a car drawing up outside.

'Not expecting anyone, you said.'

'No.'

She was petrified. She spilled her drink as she put the glass down on the table and came over to me as though my very presence insured her safety. I couldn't be sure whether the footsteps I imagined walking around the drive were real or not.

Just to show her I was in business I brought out the small revolver I had in my pocket and showed it to her. Even though a child star, who had probably handled one on the stage, she was impressed.

'Is it loaded?'

'Yes,' I lied.

'What do you want me to do?' Her eyes had that brightness of expectancy that gave me the idea that all women under eighteen were born nymphomaniacs.

'Go upstairs and stay there while I scout round to see who the intruders are.'

'Will you come with me? I don't like it upstairs, it's dark and . . . I'm frightened.'

Because she looked it I signalled her to get moving and lead the way up. Barefooted she was silent and I was careful to make even less noise. At the top of the marble flight she turned left and went down a corridor, then into a room. I followed her and found myself in one of those bedrooms they use in the best French traditional sex films. A brass double bed, about the size of Place Pigalle, was pushed into one corner of the room, over it, draped down from the ceiling an embroidered mosquito net, on the floor the usual octagonal red tiles, partly covered by a moth eaten leopard skin and all around the walls, seven foot tall mirrors so that you wouldn't ever lose sight of your companion whatever you were doing.

As soon as I had come through the door she closed it and when I looked around all I could see was myself and her shape reflected seventeen different ways, all more alluring than the other. The outside shutters were shut so all the light there was came through the slats and made the leopard think he was a tiger. There was no furniture other than the bed and she headed straight for it.

'We'll have to sit on this,' she said innocently pulling back the mosquito net. Behind the mesh curtain the bed looked invitingly comfortable. It was one of those beds which were never used for sleeping.

Taking a deep breath and loosening my collar I moved to the window instead and tried to look down at the garden through the slats. All I could see was one of the tired palm trees, a couple of green lemons on the lemon tree and a few dusty vegetables.

'If you want to have a look at the front

of the house there's a room through there,' she said. She was sitting in the middle of the bed with her knees tucked under her chin. She looked about nine now but still pretty sexy. I made a mental note to see my psychiatrist about my Humbert Humbert complexes.

'Where?' I asked. Wherever I looked all I could see was me or this elfin blonde inviting me to rape her.

'Just there, in front of you!'

After a few seconds I discovered two hinges, went towards the mirror and pushed. Nothing happened. Impatient, as young people are, the girl slipped off the bed and joined me. She kept remarkably close to me and I breathed in the sweet smell of her unscented body which had been roasted in the sun.

After a moment she found what had been a door knob, dug her small nails into the side of the door and pulled. In front of us was a room, completely dark. She stepped into the darkness, scratched around for a while, then suddenly threw open an unexpected window.

The glare of the bright sunlight that

shot in and blinded me made me turn away just as she gave out a piercing scream. I looked back in her direction, but she was on me like a leach, clutching me like a terrified child. Gripping her just as strongly I moved forward to have a look at what she had seen. Down in the street, ten or so feet below, all there was to frighten anyone was a dark blue saloon with no one in it and the sound of someone coming in through the front entrance.

Like any dramatic hero I turned to face the door and, still holding onto my clutching ingenue, moved forward so that I would have the advantage over anyone that came into the bedroom. Somehow I managed to reach for my revolver and though I had no bullets and knew that the trigger had been jammed since I had tried to use it as a bottle opener, I felt it might stop any well-wisher from doing damage.

Whoever it was took a long time finding us, long enough for little April to relax a bit and look my face over carefully. Whatever she saw there must have excited her because she pressed her dark limbs closer to me and nearly made me forget what I was being paid for.

It was just as I looked down at her, to give her an encouraging grin, that I noticed her pyjama top was ripped down the front and she was exposing all that any frenzied idiot would want to see. It was at exactly the same moment that one of the bedroom mirrors flew open and three men came in looking at me as though they had expected to find me there.

April made a big act of breaking away from me, as though it was I who was clinging on to her for dear life. Modestly she moved away from me pulling her thin garment across herself and looking so shy and innocent that no one would believe that she had deliberately torn her own clothes to land me in this beautiful position.

I didn't hold my little insignificant gun up any more, but slowly put it back into my pocket as the three men crossed the room and came towards me. They didn't look pleased, they didn't think I was nice, and I knew it would take a very long time for me to explain what I had been doing.

April, sitting on the edge of the bed made sure that I didn't catch her eye. She knew as well as I did that none of these men had come to harm her. She knew it because her scream had summoned them up from where they were waiting and I guessed all this because all three of them were in police uniform.

10

The three gentlemen weren't rough. Two of them grabbed me by the arms, twisted them at the elbows a bit, kicked me in the shins, to make me understand that from now on I was no longer my own master, and allowed their companion to search each of my pockets.

Disappointed that the gun was jammed and not loaded, but sympathising with the poor girl I had apparently violated, they bundled me out of the mirrored bedroom down the marble stairs, through the wrought iron gate, out into the front garden and into the back of the limousine.

By now a hundred or so locals had gathered at the gates and the police gave them their expected thrill. They shielded my face from view with a black scarf, snarled at the crowd, snarled at me and the one who drove crashed his gears impressively and shot down the hill at a speed which rivalled the President's own chauffeur.

Away from the onlookers my two guards relaxed and I looked at one then the other before asking my first question. 'Who sent for you?' I asked.

They didn't answer. They didn't answer for two reasons, they didn't want to and couldn't understand English. After a short drive into the centre of the town I was bundled out of the car and up five steps that led to the door of the building which housed Monsieur le Commissaire de Police.

This gentleman was a rotund character with fat cheeks, a greasy skin, a small black moustache and a uniform that had seen better days when he was thinner. I wanted to tell him that he was as original as any of Graham Greene's characters but couldn't quite make it in French. Instead I said something about wanting to go back to my hotel to get my passport.

He spoke English, however, and very kindly explained the whole simple situation. His name was Gustave Blondin, his son had served under De Gaulle as a Free

French in London in 1945, he had been approached by Interpol and asked to watch the British Film location unit who were shooting inland from Cannes and specially to keep an eye out for Miss April Mundy, the film star, who had recently bought a villa in the village.

He had then received an anonymous phone call, whom he believed to be Interpol also but wasn't sure, telling him that Miss Mundy was at her villa and that an ill wisher was going to call on her and that this intruder should be arrested as soon as possible. This task had been carried out quickly and efficiently and as I was English, or posing as such, I would have to wait for someone in a higher official capacity than himself to release me.

Though I attempted to protest, he waved a big hand in my face and suggested that I should remember that I had been caught red-handed molesting a woman of tender years which was understandable but quite unforgivable. During all this explanation I was not allowed to say a word, even tell them who

I was, or smoke a cigarette. The three brutes who had brought me in shared a bottle of 'rouge' behind my back and smiled at their chief every time they thought he was paying them a compliment.

When he at last finished his recital I opened my mouth to speak but he suggested I should keep all my strength for defending myself when the British agent of Interpol arrived — he at least might be able to make minor decisions. I breathed a sigh of relief, at least a fellow countryman would listen and not invent.

Without being asked whether this suited me or not, I was led from the Commissaire's office down a few stone steps to the back of the house. The back door which led into a gravelled garden was open and I was led out, past the Commissaire's wife who was finishing lunch with a couple of friends, past a sleeping dog and a small boy on a tricycle, through an opening in some bushes to a small, very small, circular building with a thick door and a barred window. This, I gathered was the local prison and I was pushed into it without any ceremony at all.

A bolt was jarred into a socket, three keys were turned in three separate locks and I was left to examine my medieval cell. The walls had been white a very long time ago but now were brown with damp and unmentionable use, no one had written anything funny on them or drawn anything crude. There was a hard wooden bench, a distorted bucket with a hole and above me approximately five hundred cobwebs.

If I had been desperate to get out and not frightened of spiders I could have dislodged a few of the tiles in the conical roof and got out that way, but for the moment I was quite happy to sit down and think things over.

On the back of the door, just below the grill was a rusty nail, on this I hung my jacket and tie and tried to keep as still and cool as possible. The great discomfort was not having eaten, not having drunk and having to listen to the chatter of the three women who were doing themselves well with a couple of litres of local wine.

I couldn't hear all they were saying and what I could hear I couldn't necessarily understand, but I gathered that the one who had her back to me, a big fat black back with a bun of grey hair at the top, was the hostess and presumably Monsieur le Commissaire's wife.

The Commissaire, who ate late, or ate late that day because of me, eventually sauntered out into the garden and sat down at the check linen cloth covered table. After picking his teeth, sucking the pickings and helping himself to a dollop of wine, he explained to them all about me. 'L'Anglais, criminelle! Une petite, si jeune! Apreel Mandee . . . vedette . . . film star . . . ' It was the best story he had ever been able to tell since his promotion, it would last him the rest of his life, and I could tell by the interest he was getting even from his old bag of a wife that I was going to be in for a rough time, just for the sake of the story telling.

After an hour of chop licking — he had a salad Nicoise, eleven slices of salami, twenty-four black olives, two sticks of french bread, a fried trout, another stick of french bread, two veal escalopes, sauté potatoes and more salad, a chunk of cheese the size of his fist, four glasses of rouge, two glasses of blanc, two small tots of cognac, a baba au rhum, and another tot of cognac — he remembered my existence and came over to see what I was up to.

'You want eat?'

'Oui, beaucoup. Tres soif,' I said.

'Soif! Nom de Dieu . . . vous m'excuserez.'

He had one of those comic accents from further along the coast which went with the disarming expression. He was genuinely sorry that I had been left to die and hurried over to the table to get one of the bottles which had only had one glass poured out of it.

In the door, just below the grill was a small panel which he unlocked from outside and slid open. Through it he handed me the bottle of wine and a glass.

'I am not supposed to ask questions but . . . the girl, what is she like, you know her?'

'Great friend,' I said. 'Very great friend.

You made a mistake.'

He shrugged his shoulders, he had done his duty and that was all that mattered.

'What were you going to do, eh? The bed. What an opportunity, eh? I should have told my men to wait, mmm?'

I didn't commit myself. The hot sun and the wine and the good food and no doubt the sight of his fat wife had all been too much for his imagination. He was very sorry that I hadn't been able to fulfil whatever had been my desire.

'They still hang people in England?' he asked, troubled by a noble thought.

'Only if you kill someone.'

'Ah! Mmmm. You like andouilles?'

From behind him his wife appeared carrying a plate full of greyish looking slices which I had seen him eating along with the salami. I was so hungry I didn't care what it called itself or even its description which he insisted giving me as I chewed the pressed, dried, salted intestines of his friend Marius's old pig which they had killed together a fortnight ago because it had a growth in its liver.

The pieces of andouilles stuck in my throat along with the seven black olives I was given and the stick of french bread, but I managed to wash it all down with the litre of blanc and felt better.

One of the uniformed gentlemen who had helped me out of April's villa and into the car suddenly appeared and, in an agitated state, whispered something to the Commissaire. The latter put on his worried face, excused himself and walked back up the garden path to the house. When he next appeared he was fully clothed with his kepi and baton, was accompanied by two of his gendarmes and I guessed my execution was nigh. 'The man from Interpol has arrived. He has congratulated me warmly on my achievement. The French police are more advanced in their methods of detection than he realized!'

I was marched out of the cell, back through the gravelled garden, past the three ladies who were now busy knitting — les tricoteuses — into the hallway, up the stone stairs and into the Commissaire's office.

Standing by the window, to the left of the desk, was a tall man I had met before. He turned round, smiled, then laughed in my face. Furrows seemed quite delighted to see me.

'I thought it would be you. I gather Miss Mundy was at home.'

'Yes,' I said, a great deal more pleased to see him than I thought I could be.

We both sat down while the Commissaire fluttered about like a moth round a television screen. Furrows hardly bothered to explain the situation to him and even went as far as asking the poor man to give me back my revolver. The Commissaire realized that some dreadful mistake had been made and when we left the house he ordered his two gendarmes to open the car door for me and even give me a salute.

Furrows, who had every intention of enjoying his short stay in the South of France, asked the driver to take us to the nearest bistro overlooking the sea and, on a sun drenched terrace, I joined him to eat a quite magnificent steak and polish off a bottle of chilled Rosé.

The situation was not one over which

he could lose much time, but since I had located April and she was presumably still in the house where I had found her, he could give himself the time to enjoy a good meal and a bit of sunshine, especially as he would have to take her back to England the moment he saw her. Though he refused to say so she was obviously his Number One suspect.

On arriving Furrows had sent his Sergeant to keep an eye on the VILLA AVRIL and after two coffees and a brandy we moved off to find out how he had got on.

Outside the tall white house, the crowd that had been there to see me being taken away by the French police was still there — only larger. The Press boys had got wind of a story and a number of cars were parked outside the tall black gates.

Monsieur le Commissaire was there in person to see that no one had entered the property and when he saw us arriving he doubled his efforts to please me and actually opened the car door for us himself.

Inside the courtyard, sitting on the

head of a stone dolphin was Furrows's Sergeant, waiting. From his expression we gathered that the bird had flown but we also guessed that he knew where she had gone.

'Left as soon as Mr. Flute was taken away, sir. Someone called for her, a man wearing dark glasses, a red baseball cap, lime green shirt and blue trousers.'

'I wonder who *that* could be,' I said.

'Oscar Lovaks, her father.' Sometimes Furrows didn't have a sense of humour.

'Any idea where they might have gone?' I asked, to show that I was just as much in the case as anyone else.

'In the Basses Alpes somewhere, sir, near a village called Saint Chauflusse, that's where they're making the film.'

'It figures,' Furrows mumbled.

'Dead keen on getting his film finished, is Lovaks,' I added.

'Where exactly is this place, far?'

'Not as the crow flies, sir, some twenty-five to thirty miles, but it's a winding road and takes a good . . . two hours.'

'Two hours!'

'It's arid country, sir, desert, the road is more of a track.'

'How well off are the French police for transport?'

I left Furrows to discuss how he would get to Miss Mundy in her safe location spot and wandered off into the garden. I made friends with a small lizard and the point of a cactus, tried to work out what my next move would be and realized that I hadn't been much help to anybody. I would have to square things off with Zeelah and settle a small account with Pascale and Lovaks, but before I could decide exactly how I would go about this, Furrows joined me.

'Lovaks wanted you to find his daughter, didn't he?'

'Yes.'

'Then you'd better find her, hadn't you? And when you do, get her to talk, will you? We've got nothing on her at all except that she was the first to act suspiciously. Until she reveals something about herself or someone else . . . we haven't much power to do anything.'

I was astounded. Here was the Yard

asking me to do their work for them. My expression must have conveyed my surprise.

'Why don't I go after her?' Furrows asked. 'Because if I do the Press will start yapping — it's your unimportance that's valuable, Flute, if you would help.'

'How can I refuse? Where will I find her?'

'We'll get the exact location of the unit, we'll find you transport and anything else you want. Meanwhile, what are you doing this afternoon?'

'Nothing special.'

'Good, we'll leave this dump in the capable hands of my Sergeant and go to Cannes. It might be more stimulating to make plans.' He paused to light a cigarette, then added, 'You haven't a spare pair of bathing trunks I could borrow, and some suntan lotion?'

* * *

I was rubbing three liquid ounces of Ambre Solaire between the shoulder blades of one of those tall athletic model girls they manufacture in Sweden when Furrows's Sergeant found us.

Furrows, white skinned and sporting a pair of knobbly knees, had struck up a rapid friendship with the model's friend, a Danish girl who was going to London as an au pair and who wanted a permit to work. He wasn't at all pleased that his assistant had been so quick and efficient.

'The film unit has been located, sir . . . I have all the information in the car.'

'Good,' he said, disassociating himself as much as he could from the silver haired doll who was toying with the hairs on his chest. 'Any idea how long they'll be there?'

'At least a week, sir, they haven't started filming at all so one of the reporters said. It's very hot apparently and you have to take your own water supply.'

'We'll meet you in the bar of the hotel presently. Have a drink on me while you're waiting.'

The Sergeant needed no second invitation, glanced at me and the shoulder blades between my two massaging hands and raised his eyebrows.

'Want to make a takeover bid?' I suggested.

He smiled, sprinted off but looked back several times. As I worked on the twelfth vertebra of the Swede's backbone, I tried to tell her how wonderful our British policemen were. It was the least I could do considering they were sending me into the depths of the Gobi desert.

11

Lovaks's film location was as well organized as any army field day operation. Seventy or eighty people were involved including the camera crews, the make-up artists, the truck drivers, the cooks, the electricians, the clapper boy, continuity girl, Uncle Tom Cobley and all. I got to them by jeep with my own driver who knew his way about these parts.

The place was like the Arizona desert, or the Sierras or any of those places one was told looked like deserts by the movie kings. The location was suitable for a Western, a gold rush epic or a hand grenade battle between the Desert Rats and German Panzers, but in actual fact it was going to be used as a background for Miss Noelle Knowles supposedly looking for the remains of an Egyptian tomb.

While dusting the corner stone of a pyramid, dressed in white shirt and white shorts, she was going to come across an oil well and get a load of black grease shot in her face. As the female Miss Knowles was portraying couldn't stand dirt she would be forced to tear off her blackened garments and run stark naked through the desert chased by this oil geyser.

Everyone was looking forward to shooting this scene because it meant that only one person really worked — the actress. Though, of course, there were a few preliminaries before she started dusting the desert floor, like laying the oil pipe — a plastic hose leading from the decided spot to a large water truck filled with black ink, guaranteed to ruin any white clothes at a distance of fifty yards — and the erection of a gantry providing the cameras with a bird's eye view of the incident.

When I reached the location spot I stopped at the sight of two canvas armchairs. One had the name 'OSCAR LOVAKS' stencilled on the back, the other 'JUSTIN JOYCE'. Both were empty. Inside a tent nearby I could see a worn out secretary typing away, probably rewriting the script. Seven electricians sat at the foot of a battery of arc lamps watching seven props men adjusting the pipe line. Three caravans were parked some five hundred yards from the centre of activity and I guessed that April would be resting in one of them.

Dressed in a white topee, yellow shirt, blue trousers and brown sandals, also sporting dark glasses, I didn't attract any attention. Leaving my driver and the jeep I walked some distance on the rocky ground to the largest of the caravans and climbed up the three steel steps to the open door.

Inside, four chairs had been arranged to face a panel of mirrors. In two of them sat two women, hot, clammy, tired women wearing pink nylon overalls and smelling of grease paint. I didn't ask them who they were, their thick make-up and surroundings alone told me.

'Miss Mundy?'

'The green caravan — Number three.'

'What's next on the schedule?'

'What schedule?' The one that spoke was American. 'No one's done anything yet and we've been here a week!'

'A week?'

'Yeah. Delays brother, delays. We lost our star, did you know that? Shot himself or something, way back in limey country. The nut!'

'Tell me more.'

'Can't, don't know any more. You with the unit?'

'Not exactly — publicity.'

'Oh, I should hang around, they're hoping to shoot the oil well scene. Two of the girls do a striptease or something.'

'Two?'

'Yeah, Noelle Knowles and April Mundy . . . '

I took it that both girls got drenched in the black oil or something. But I wasn't here to enjoy myself. Leaving the painted ladies I made my way to the green caravan with its 'No. 3' clearly painted on the side.

Inside, everything was cosy and English. Chintz curtains, chintz bed covers on the bunks, chintz chair upholstery, chintz wallpaper — the lot. Home from home for little girls, only no little girl was in the vehicle. Instead, lying on one of the bunks dressed in a new kimono type pair of pyjamas was my old friend and client — Zeelah Danton.

She didn't show signs of recognition till I took my glasses and pith helmet off, even then she couldn't believe it was me.

Without being asked I sat down on the other bunk, wiped my sunglasses slowly with a lily-white handkerchief and stuck them back on my nose.

'I'm sorry I've been so long in reporting, Mrs. Danton, but you didn't leave a forwarding address, as you said you would.'

'What are you doing here?'

'Watching over your daughter, like you asked me to do.'

She was really stuck for words, she was so unprepared for me that I could read the situation like a book. She raised herself on her elbows, then after making quite sure she was awake, swung her remarkably young legs to the floor and stood up.

'How did you get here?'

'Jeep. I got it at cut price, but I'll still have to charge you the best part of fifty pounds for the hiring of it.'

'I didn't mean that.'

'What did you mean?' My tone was sharp because I felt that way. The jigsaw in mind was still full of little unrecognized pieces, but she was looming up a bit bigger than the others and I imagined she could fit in the bottom left hand corner of the whole thing.

'I meant that . . . that . . . '

'You're surprised to see me at all?'

'Yes.'

'Why?'

'I wasn't expecting you.'

'Is that a fact?'

Unprompted I suddenly got up, reached for the door and slammed it shut. We were alone, in the small area of a caravan, in a heat of two hundred centigrade and she was seven inches away from me with her back to one of the bunks. With gentlemanly politeness I gave her a push which forced her to sit down. I then sat down myself opposite her and looked her fair and square in the face.

'Shall we recap?' I suggested.

She was a little frightened, a little worried, a little bit uncomfortable because I was holding both her wrists in a vice-like grip.

'When you hired me to find out whether Oscar Lovaks and Noelle Knowles were having an affair, you knew all the time that they were — didn't you?'

'No. I knew that something was going on under the guise of publicity — but I wasn't sure.'

'Why did you want Justin to hear the truth?'

She looked away embarrassed. Whatever she was going to tell me was going to be a lie, so I didn't give her time to think up a good one.

'Why did you want Justin to know that his wife was having an affair with Oscar?'

'I loved him, I didn't want him to get hurt.'

'When you say hurt, you mean emotionally?'

'Yes.'

'He got hurt plenty physically though, didn't he?'

'Don't be cruel.'

She turned her head away as though I had slapped her. I had a good mind to, but my tight grip was enough to keep her under control.

'Who did it?'

'I don't *know*!'

'You've no idea?'

'No. Please, I'd like you to leave now. I'd like you to stop working for me . . . I'll pay whatever . . . '

'You can't my darling, you can't just switch off the current like that. You've involved me in a murder and you've involved me in such a way that the police are interested in my life history. You know who they suspect?'

'April?'

'No,' I lied. It was strange that everyone was suspecting April.

'Who?'

'You!' I said, letting go of her red wrists.

It sent a cold shower down her spine. She twitched, crossed her legs and looked around for a cigarette.

'Now *I* know you didn't do it, don't I?'

'Yes.'

'Do I?' I whipped off my glasses and looked at her with my sex hungry psychiatric look. '*Do* I know you didn't do it?'

'Of course! You don't think . . . '

'You were in the studio at the time.'

'But why should I hurt Justin?'

'Why should you suspect your own daughter?' I wasn't going to give her a chance.

'I don't, but the police do.'

'Why should they?'

'Because . . . because she hated Justin.'

'Is that what you told the Yard before coming down here?'

'Yes.'

'Why did she hate him?'

She got to her feet, opened a small cupboard and reached for a packet of cigarettes.

'You haven't got a teenage daughter, have you?'

'Not yet.'

'They're complex creatures, specially when they've been brought up by irresponsible parents like Oscar and myself.'

184

This was going to be one of those 'mea culpa' stories so I leaned over, threw the door open to get a little air into the place and leaned back on my chintz cushion.

'When Oscar and I divorced, April didn't mind too much. It was a change for her and fun, she spent half her time with me, half her time with him, and was exceedingly spoilt by both of us. When I married Justin I lost interest in her, naturally — at least that's how she saw it. Justin was nearer to her age group than mine, I hadn't up to then taken much notice of pop records, the twist . . . any of her interests, and because of him I suddenly did. She couldn't swallow that.'

She put her unlit cigarette in her mouth and waited for me to light it for her. My pockets were sticky with heat and the lighter didn't work, by the time she had found some matches she was more composed.

'But when Justin left you for Noelle, what then?' I asked.

'She hated him even more — for making me unhappy.'

'That's why she killed him?'

'She didn't! But it's a motive and the only one the police have got on anyone. That's why we're afraid.'

'We? You and who? Oscar?'

She had slipped, it didn't matter much to me, but it mattered to her.

'I think you owe me an explanation, Miss Danton,' I said standing up. I looked taller when I stood up.

'What about?'

'About you not telling me that you knew where April had gone, about you not telling me that you planned with Oscar to have me as a scapegoat.'

'I *didn't*!'

I was feeling lousy, the heat was nearly unbearable. I was aware that I was losing time, yet didn't want to give up this opportunity of possibly finding out more about Lovaks's crazy set-up.

'When you asked me to find your daughter, did you know where she was?'

'No!'

'But you had contacted Oscar.'

'He contacted me. As soon as he heard that Justin had been murdered he rang me up to tell me April had disappeared and that the police would probably suspect her. She was the only one who could have done it and had a motive.'

'He rang you up you say?'

'Yes.'

'Yet both of you were at the studios when it happened.'

She gave me an odd look, a look which told me she hadn't been aware that Oscar was at the BBC at the time of the murder. I remembered seeing her leave soon after the incident so just waited for her to answer.

'I left as soon as I heard that the rehearsal had been abandoned. You remember . . . you saw me!'

'You believed Oscar anyway, you believed that April could have done it.'

'Yes. That's why I called you. After I left the house to go to the hotel, before seeing Mr. Furrows at the Yard, I rang him.'

'What for?'

'I felt terribly alone. Needed him. I knew he had enough people organized to help April. It was then that he told me that he had sent her to the Villa Avril.'

'He didn't tell you then that he was going to try and get me arrested instead of her, presumably?'

She hesitated, bit her lower lip, stubbed out her half smoked cigarette and trembled.

'He asked me whether I thought the police might suspect you.'

'And what did you say?'

'I said I thought they might.'

'Thank you.'

I drew on my own cigarette, examined the tip, the length of the ash, played for time to make her more on edge and finally dropped the stub on the caravan floor and stepped on it.

'Was it your idea that I should be caught raping April?'

'What?'

She seemed hurt by the suggestion. Her look was one of complete bewilderment and pity, she was beginning to doubt my sanity.

'You didn't know that I had been sent by Oscar to the Villa Avril and that there I was arrested by the police.'

'For breaking and entering . . . surely . . .'

'Not quite.'

Her features relaxed into a smile. She shrugged her shoulders and sighed deeply.

'I've never fully understood Oscar, that's why we divorced. He has mad ideas, wild ideas, but some of them have payed off so well that . . . you just can't stop him. I'm sorry you should have been one of his pawns.'

'You don't think that one of his wild ideas might have been to kill Justin?'

'Maybe? You never know with him.'

She seemed remarkably unconcerned now, as though the fatigue of the last few days had been enough punishment for anything she might have done.

'How is it that you're here?' I asked.

'Oscar gave me a job, a small part, I wanted to be down here with April. She still relies on me a bit you know, and funnily enough so does Oscar. We were married for eleven years.'

Through the open door I could see some activity going on around the hose-pipe. Suddenly a powerful jet of water spurted up in the air and drenched a few of the technicians. The assistant director got out his megaphone, bawled out instructions to a section of the unit and I stood up to have a better look.

'Who took care of April when the police arrested me. Oscar?'

'Yes.'

'He had to bring her here at all costs to continue filming, I suppose. Film first, feelings after. Where is April now?'

I was looking for her in the small crowd of people that was moving towards the camera gantry.

'No one knows. They never got here.'

12

I thought of Furrows and his Sergeant and the two Scandinavians, and the good time they were all having in the cool deep blue Mediterranean. I thought of Scotland Yard and the policemen all in their hot uniforms talking about Furrows's luck. I thought of the Commissionaire waiting for the results of Furrows's enquiries before asking for promotion and of the Government officials waiting for April's arrest, and I thought of April who was now somewhere with her mad father who himself might be the killer.

I left Zeelah in her oven warm caravan and walked out into the furnace hot heat of the desert. Lorries were driving to an area where the arc lamps and more cameras had been placed, people were shouting at each other and I headed for this particular scene of activity hoping I'd find someone or something which might enlighten me as to April's whereabouts.

The chair with Lovaks's name on it was still empty, but Justin's was not. Miss Noelle Knowles herself was sitting in it, so I sat myself down in the producer's throne and tickled the back of the gold brown neck and the gold blonde cropped curls above it. She turned round annoyed.

'Good Lord! What are you doing here?' She was surprised to say the least.

'Hanging around, looking for a story or something.'

'You still pretending to be a reporter?'

'I am a reporter, of sorts. Where's the big man?'

'No one knows.'

'Hasn't he been here at all?'

'Yesterday. Then he went off to get his precious daughter and hasn't come back.'

'Maybe he's been arrested.'

'Maybe.'

She was quite radiant with the solid sun blazing behind her casting a silver line round her silhouette. There were no tears in her eyes, or red circles round the rims, or dark patches under them, she was as fresh and as beautiful as the day she got married. A merry widow if I ever saw one.

'No regrets?'

'Not particularly. What should I be having regrets about?'

'Your husband died recently, remember?'

'Oh that! He had it coming to him.'

'That's a pretty damning statement. Who from?'

'Don't you know?' It was a sly question, an over the shoulder question with a slight smile playing on her lips.

'No, tell me.'

'I thought you came to get her.'

'April.'

'Who else?'

'Why should she kill your husband?'

'He was her stepfather. She didn't like him.'

'Hardly a reason.'

'That and the dramatic way she did it. Little idiot!'

'You liked her?'

'How would you feel about someone who killed one of your favourite relations?'

'Favourite. You're not exactly in mourning.'

'Why should I be? That's all a lot of hypocritical show for relatives. I can't say I was head over heels in love with him, but he had his good points.'

'Do you inherit anything?'

'That's my business, isn't it?'

She had been watching the technicians preparing the acting area like a tennis fan watching players at Wimbledon, but suddenly her attention was drawn by a cloud of dust which appeared in the distance along the road. One by one the technicians saw the cloud and they stopped work to look up. In the cloud was an engine and when the noise took the shape of an army lorry a small cheer went up.

'Here he comes! I hope he's got her with him.'

'If he hasn't?'

'I suppose he'll scrap this scene. It's all based round her. The whole story was a rewrite to fit her in anyway. And now Mum's joined the merry party.'

The lorry, a big six wheeler traction job with only the cabin and no trailer came to a halt outside a tent some hundred feet from us. Though I was occupying his chair I didn't move and neither did blondy Knowles.

'Seems as though he didn't find her,' I said, looking at a solitary Lovaks getting out of the truck, 'but he's brought a substitute.'

'What do you mean?'

With interest I watched Noelle's reaction as she watched with astonishment a small, dark, slim girl being helped out of the cabin by the assistant director. She was still wearing white trousers, but they were made of linen.

Noelle half rose to make sure she had seen right, then sat down again with a bump. Her eyes were blazing and the grip she had on the arm of the chair was tight enough to squeeze the juice out of the wood.

'Miss Anjoux, I believe,' I said to encourage her annoyance.

'The bitch!'

'Oh why? I think she's quite delightful.'

'You would! I bet she's wormed her way into April's part. If she has I'm walking out!'

No one heard her say that except me, but when the members of the unit saw Pascale they instinctively turned to look at Noelle. Lovaks sensed this reaction and glanced towards Noelle knowing that he would have to face the music sooner or later. What he didn't expect was to have to face me.

He didn't exactly do a double take, he glanced at Noelle, turned to speak to his assistant, then froze. After eight or nine seconds he slowly turned again to make sure it was my smiling mug he had seen.

After a moment or two of careful thinking he walked towards us and a deathly hush fell on the company. While crossing the hundred odd feet that lay between us he made up his mind to ignore me, one thing only mattered to him for the moment, the film.

'I . . . couldn't find her,' he said to Noelle.

'So you're replacing her with Pascale?' she said to him.

'Yeah. I thought I would. We've wasted enough time already.'

'Are you leaving the part as it was

written for April?'

'Why not? Can't afford to make any more changes now.'

'Why not? Because it means Pascale will be the star. I can wear it with your daughter, Oscar, but not with her!'

'Mmmm!' It was a grunt, confirmation of what he thought she'd say, but he had the answer all ready.

'You've got your public to think of Noelle, they liked Justin, they wouldn't like his widow to be too happy-go-lucky.'

'There's nothing happy-go-lucky about my part in this film. Either Pascale doesn't play April's part or . . . '

'Yeah? Or what? Someone's got to play the kid's scenes haven't they? If it's not Pascale who will it be?'

The storm was beginning to get ugly, Lovaks had taken one hand out of his trouser pocket to express his mood, the technicians came a little nearer and Pascale came a bit more into view.

'Find an unknown . . . I'm not fussy.'

'Not much! Pascale isn't famous you know, one film!'

'She's known enough. There's a big

difference between her and April, and you know it.'

'I do? Well, you spell it out for me, because I don't quite understand what you're talking about.'

'Sex, honey. S E X. Pascale will be a direct rival. April isn't. She isn't even a nymphette.'

'No?'

'No. That's why I don't mind her.'

'You don't mind April taking the part because she's got no sex appeal, is that it?' Lovaks repeated, just to make sure.

'That's it. She has a childlike sex appeal, but she isn't mature enough to use it.'

'Ha!'

The small exclamation was from Pascale who had reached the argument now and was standing a few feet behind Lovaks. 'You, you keep out of this!' Noelle was getting really warm.

'Why should I? I'm involved, my big chance is at stake, isn't it Oscar darling?'

The french accent grated on Noelle's nerves like barbed wire fencing on a greyhound's back. Oscar darling showed signs of enjoyment and lit up the stub of an extinguished cigar.

'And what, sweet innocent Miss, was that exclamation meant to imply anyway?'

'It was meant to imply, Miss Knowles — I'm sorry, *Mrs.* Joyce, that your view of April's childlike innocence wasn't exactly your husband's.'

'Oh?' Noelle was puzzled, the unit awed, I was intrigued.

The two girls were looking at each other as though there wasn't too much mutual admiration between them.

'Right, let's drop it shall we?' Lovaks was bored or worried.

'I would just like that last remark explained,' Noelle suggested tensely.

'Yeah, well I don't think it'll lead anyone anywhere.' Lovaks was tense. I had never seen him so tense before, he seemed to be very worried by the turn of events.

'I would like that last remark explained, if you don't mind.' Noelle was moving forward now towards Pascale and looking pretty nasty.

'You're a blonde, Noelle darling. Justin

liked blondes. April was a blonde, too
— only younger!'

'Are you suggesting that April and
Justin . . . '

'Why not? April is seventeen next
month, I'm seventeen myself.' Casually
Pascale moved toward Oscar, took his
hand in hers and squeezed it. 'Aren't I?'

'Did you know about this Oscar?' It
was Noelle, white with rage.

'I found out.'

'Why didn't you do something about
it?'

'I did. I put Pascale onto him.'

★   ★   ★

The riot that followed made up for all the
waiting in the intense heat which the film
unit had had to do during the past few
weeks.

A long time ago in some North
England town I had seen a cockfight
when the livelier of the two birds had
lunged out with outstretched claw and
torn its opponent apart. Noelle didn't
quite ruin Pascale's innocent features

but she tried pretty hard. The small brunette was surprisingly lithe and obviously had had a few lessons in Judo for within seconds she had thrown the taller blonde and both rolled about in the dust. After several blood curdling screams and more oaths Pascale got Noelle on her back, straddled her and then gave her a couple of back handed slaps which were enough to make me wince.

The assistant director waited for the right moment before moving in with a few of the camera boys, and separated the two girls. They were, as far as the film was concerned, valuable property.

During it all Lovaks chewed on the end of his cigar stub and met my steady gaze. For me the episode virtually held the answer to the murder.

'I'll take you to her, now,' he said.

It sounded like an invitation I should refuse. He knew I suspected him, he knew I would go to the police, what better than to rub me out.

'What about the film, can you spare the time?'

'This trip will save me time — if you play ball.'

'Again.'

We looked at each other as men do when they're weighing up vital circumstances in their lives. I couldn't stay in the desert all my life, if he wanted to kill me he'd find a way sooner or later. It was a gamble, if I won I'd get to April, if I lost, I'd get to Justin. *He'd* answer a few of my questions anyway.

As we headed for the truck a groan went up from the members of the unit. Though most of them were getting paid overtime, double time and making a fortune, they were bored and hot.

Lovaks climbed into the driver's seat, nearly broke the gear lever trying to get it into first and we started off with a few rib shaking jerks. The drive out of the desert valley and up to the main road wasn't too exciting. Lovaks hadn't driven the lorry much and was concentrating all his attention on how to handle it. Now, I realized, was not the time to ask any questions or try probing deeper into his odd mind.

'Far from here?' I asked as he turned left on the tarmacked road, now heading towards Grasse.

'Couple of miles.'

He was thinking hard about something, concerned about my presence in his life maybe. The road was straight for a while though dangerously sandwiched between a cliff on one side and a precipice on the other.

'How long have you known April was going around with Justin?' I asked.

'Why?'

'I'm interested.'

'I don't think it's really any of your business.'

I didn't like his tone, I didn't like the way he was gripping the steering wheel either. We were doing fifty at least and the needle of the speedometer couldn't go any higher. To stop myself worrying I looked down to my right and stared at the road whizzing past. There was no door between me and the road, and no wall between the road and the drop.

'Supposing I told you I thought you did it?' he said suddenly, glancing quickly in my direction, then concentrating on a hairpin bend.

'What motive would I have had?'

'Money. Zeelah could have paid you.'

It was an interesting thought, one that had never occurred to me.

'Why should she want him out of the way?'

'She had plenty to reproach Justin, no woman likes being told she's old. Besides he had money.'

'He made a will in her favour?'

'They had a joint account. She's no fool, she made that boy, she worked hard to get him where he was. He was beginning to ask for some of it back.'

'Good story,' I said. 'The police would think it a strong enough motive but yours would be just as strong.'

'Mine?'

He jammed on the brakes and I went forward. My head struck the windscreen — but neither broke. It was a warning, from now on I would have to tread more carefully.

'What do you mean, mine?'

'You could have killed Joyce, very easily.'

'For what?'

'He was friends with your daughter.'

'Don't make me laugh. Why should I care what he did with her, him or any other man. I'm no hypocrite, Flute, I know the girl's got sex appeal, that's why she'll be a great star. He wasn't the first anyway.'

He was driving fast again, going down hill towards the village of Mardouxpuis. He was grinning at what I had mentioned and I was trying to work out how genuine that grin was.

'Look, Flute, if that's the way you're thinking, maybe you're not the man for this job.'

'What job?'

'I want you to take April to Tangiers, and hide her and look after her till I get shot of this film and can take over from you without raising any suspicions.'

'Why do you want April hidden?'

'Because *she* killed Justin, that's why.'

He was lying. I knew he was lying but I didn't know why. I couldn't believe that he'd try to make his own daughter take the rap for a crime he had committed, and yet. Suddenly we swung off the main road and started climbing a steep uneven track. The truck found this heavy going but had to cope with even worse ground when the track ended and we bumped across a field.

After a mile or so, raising clouds of dust behind us, we went down an unexpectedly steep slope in the hollow of which stood a derelict farmhouse.

'This is it,' Lovaks said, stopping the engine and climbing out energetically.

I followed, for the first time wondering whether I had any future. He was trying to hide a grin and I was trying to look confident. The moment I stepped into that house anything might happen and no one would find me for a long, long time.

As we got to the front of the farmhouse I realized it was even more derelict than I had at first thought. There were no windows, no doors, no roof, a good enough hiding place for the body of a Private Detective, but not an ideal spot to serve as refuge for your own daughter.

'You find some dainty places for her,' I said.

'Beggars aren't choosers.'

We got to what had been the main entrance and he led the way inside. An old staircase rose straight in front of us and he started climbing. At the top of the stairs he paused to make sure I was following him, when I had joined him on the landing he turned right down a short corridor and paused again, this time in front of a closed door.

'April?' he asked in a loud whisper.

The door opened and we both stood and looked aghast at the unexpected man who was grinning at us. Furrows in the company of his Sergeant and no one else.

'Good afternoon Mr. Lovaks, your daughter left about an hour ago with one of my men.'

Lovaks was staggered. He had never written this part of the script.

'What are you going to do with her?'

'Take her back to England.'

'But why?'

'She confessed.'

'She what?'

He was stunned. Suddenly he turned on me and gripped me by the collar.

'He did it! He did it!' He had a powerful enough grip.

'No, Mr. Lovaks, Mr. Flute has been working for us for some time now, and we're quite sure . . . '

I didn't hear the end of Furrows's recital, all I heard was what Lovaks thought of me before he lashed out with his fifteen carat gold ring at my face.

'You bastard!' he screamed, kicked me in the stomach, jarred me with his elbow and tried a double handed rabbit punch.

Twice I ducked, hit back, grabbed hold of his neck and twisted him round. We fell to the floor, rolled over a couple of times in the direction of the stairs, then he fell on me from nowhere as I tried to get up. I could have hit the banisters, or the wall, or even Furrows who was wondering just when to step in, but I didn't. I took a headlong dive into oblivion above the fourteen worm eaten steps which didn't carry my weight and crumpled as I landed on them head first.

As I gasped with pain then warded off the falling timber with an arm, Lovaks's huge shadow jumped from the first floor, landed by the door and sprinted out to the lorry followed by the Sergeant.

When Furrows eventually got me to my feet it was only to tell me that his Sergeant had twisted both his ankles attempting to board the moving lorry and that he was now writhing in agony halfway across the field. Looking out of the door all I could see was the truck and its cloud of dust making a successful getaway.

'Haven't you got a car?'

'No. We were dropped here by helicopter and the pilot won't be back for half an hour. We've got a Thermos of tea though, if you'd like some.'

13

Five minutes before expected time a drone split the silent sky and the revolving cutters of the helicopter suddenly appeared like a locust descending.

All three of us were hauled up into the shaking cockpit while the machine hovered a few feet above the ground, then whisked up to five hundred feet like an American elevator.

Six minutes later we landed in the back garden of the Cannes Constabulary, were greeted by a number of uniformed men and led to a comfortable office where, sitting nervously on the edge of a chair, Miss April Mundy awaited our arrival.

Furrows wanted results and he wanted them quickly, with his Sergeant hors de combat and a mountain of work to do he decided to let me have the first bash at cross-examining her. He didn't care how I went about it providing I didn't torture her unduly. I could have anything except time, he was going to ring up London, get his sergeant away and replaced and by then I would have the riddle solved.

Though she had confessed to Justin's murder Furrows was far from satisfied that this was the truth. Adding to Lovaks's behaviour the facts that had emerged from the Pascale-Noelle quarrel, he favoured the girl's father as number one suspect.

What he wanted me to do was simple. Break the girl, trip her up, get a confession from her that she wasn't guilty.

My knowledge of cross-examinations was limited to what I had seen on the films and television. I didn't strike myself as being a bully, but having been hurt by Lovaks I wasn't in any mood to be lenient either. I sat down behind the big desk and stared at my victim, and some victim, I thought.

Her skin had darkened since she'd been in the South of France or maybe the room was dark, she was wearing a tight skirt with a loose linen sleeveless shirt affair. On her feet she had sandles, her toes had no nail polish. She looked good, healthy, if a little worried. Her father had certainly not used her in his film only because she was his daughter.

'All this business has got rather out of hand,' I said, offering her a cigarette.

There were no cameras around, no one to see us, just her and me alone. The relationship could be formal, informal, man and woman, or interrogator and accused. I didn't make the decision, I wanted her to choose which part she was going to play.

She said nothing but looked around. She didn't give me the impression of having any great guilt complexes.

'How long had Justin been your lover?' I tried.

She reacted. Either she didn't know I knew, or she didn't expect me to be so blunt, or, as I suspected, she was surprised by the adult terminology I used to describe their relationship.

She flicked some non-existent ash on to the floor and tried once or twice to meet my steady gaze, but she was having difficulty. Her only enemy was herself. She didn't know how to behave in these circumstances, she didn't know the rules.

'A year, two?' I prompted.

'I only left school last year!' she said.

That gave me a bit of a shock, but I made use of it. Sometimes I had to admire my own talent for making the most of unexpected situations.

'That wouldn't stop either of you, surely.'

'He was my stepfather!'

'Which means you lived in the same house. Very convenient.'

'You're being beastly! That's horrid.' The thought, for some reason appalled her. I wasn't dealing with a young nymphomaniac after all.

'You loved him?'

'Yes.'

'And he was your first great love?'

'Yes.'

'Then why did you kill him?'

She was all natural now. She got up, strolled to the window and looked out at the garden with its gravel and its helicopter and the uniformed men standing about.

'I didn't kill him,' she said, just like that.

'Do you know who did?'

'No. But Pascale Anjoux had as much reason to as I did.'

'Pascale? Why her?' I was astonished at the suggestion.

'She and Justin were friends long before he met Noelle. When she found out about me . . . she was livid!'

'Crime passionelle? Why didn't she kill *you*?'

She was sitting down again, on the edge of the chair, biting her lower lip, ignoring the french cigarette that had gone out between her long fingers.

'I think your father did it. He had far more reason than anyone else. Justin took his wife, his daughter, was married to Noelle, whom your father has a penchant for, and now you tell me, Pascale.'

'Dad was never interested in Pascale! He wouldn't lower himself to touch a girl like that!'

I had found the spot. The French girl was certainly popular. Everyone was as keen to dislike her as they were to accuse April of the murder. I wondered if there was any connection.

'Tell me,' I said gently, 'what did your father ask you to do as far as I was concerned?'

'Help frame you.'

'For what?'

'Anything, attempted murder.'

'Why?'

'To gain time, so that the police would switch their suspicions.'

'From you or from him?'

'He was never suspected.'

'I've suspected him all along. I think he killed Justin and so do you, that's why you played in this charade with me. You weren't trying to save your own skin by leading me into that trap, you were trying to save his. Everyone's been covering up for Mr. Oscar Lovaks, either because they love him or because he's their only guarantee of a steady income.'

'You're horrible!'

'Maybe.' I paused, I was nearly there but she hadn't said anything definite. 'They cut your head off in France you know, they don't hang you.'

Unintentionally she moved her head from side to side letting her long hair brush her back and shoulders.

'I wouldn't have thought he was worth it. He'd let you take the rap to save his precious film, you know that!'

She wasn't speaking, she was thinking plenty, but she wasn't going to say a word.

'He was quick enough to replace you anyway. Pascale's taking your part over, just in case they do lock you up.'

'He'd never do a thing like that!'

'He killed a man, why shouldn't he replace his daughter?'

'He killed Justin *because* of me!'

She looked up like a frightened elk. She was quite terrified of me, suddenly. She had been led into a trap, caught, and she knew that there was nothing she could do to help herself.

'I'm sorry,' I said, sympathetically, 'we would have found out sooner or later. If you'll sign a statement just telling them that it wasn't you and give us an alibi, that's all that will be required. I don't think we can ask you to accuse him outright.'

'He hated Justin, hated him since

Mummy fell in love with him . . . '

'I know,' I said. I couldn't stand anyone crying, it brought tears to my own eyes. Big sympathising act. 'I know,' I repeated putting my hand on her smooth silk shoulder. I didn't know, I didn't know anything about the complex emotions of this crazy family.

'You didn't actually see the murder?' I asked tentatively.

'No. But who else could have done it. Everyone was in the canteen.'

As far as I was concerned the interview was over. April had said as much as she could for the moment, Lovaks was our man, he had killed Justin in a fit of jealous anger, all of which was quite understandable. With his imaginative mind he had thought up various ways of getting out of it, he had accused his daughter, then tried to accuse me, he had complicated everyone's lives, including his own, by rewriting his script and recasting it as often as his film. I picked up the telephone and contacted Furrows.

★ ★ ★

When Furrows came in and April was led away I gave him the whole story. He listened patiently but not too attentively, then told me that a recording machine had taped the whole of my conversation. I was delighted that he trusted me so much and suggested that it might be a good idea if they got on with the job of finding Lovaks and making an arrest instead of wasting my time.

'You've been invaluable, my dear Flute,' Furrows said with a kind smile. 'While you've been questioning the little blonde I've been out in the field.'

The lorry, apparently, had been found abandoned not far off the main road to Cannes. Lovaks had probably hitch-hiked or got another car and done a bunk. It wouldn't be very easy for him to get far because his face was well enough known along the Cote d'Azur.

Furrows thanked me for all the help I had contributed and just asked me one more favour. His new sergeant had arrived from London by air, and he was going to round up all the people involved and take statements. He wondered whether I would go along with him to make the introductions, it would save everyone a lot of time and the Yard would remember my kindness.

Anxious to see my client Zeelah Danton again, to make sure that I wouldn't be out of pocket, I agreed to accompany the new man to the location. With luck Pascale would still be there, or if she wasn't maybe Noelle Knowles might be happy to have my company for a few hours. One could work wonders with bored film stars on a warm night.

* * *

The set was deserted. The moon was shining on the white sands and it was cool. In one tent most of the unit were playing cards and drinking wine, in another the executives were holding a meeting. Round the large table I recognized a few people, a cameraman, the assistant director, the lighting expert, the continuity girl, a weary scriptwriter playing noughts and crosses with Pascale, and Zeelah looking extremely feminine and composed. At the head of the table was someone I hadn't expected to see at all, Oscar Lovaks, himself.

He didn't seem particularly concerned when he saw me, though I noticed he had a piece of sticking plaster above a swollen right eye. I told the new Detective Sergeant that promotion seemed to be heading his way fast, and only just managed to restrain him from breaking up the happy party. We watched Lovaks very closely for signs of guilt, but there were none. A murderer who had committed a crime in a moment of passion, he was completely unmoved by his deed and only absorbed in his film, his life.

After explaining several final points to his assistant and the cameraman, he turned to us.

'Yes, gentlemen? Can I help you? Mr. Flute, I see that you have recovered.'

'Could we see you for a moment in private, sir,' the Sergeant started.

'You can, but I have nothing to hide from these people. They all know what has happened.'

The detective glanced at me, I nodded and he took the bull by the horns.

'I have to ask you to accompany me, sir, to the police station.'

'La gendarmerie you mean! For what?'

'We wish to question you about Mr. Joyce's death, sir.'

'I thought you had arrested my daughter for that.'

I felt a pain in my guts. He had planned it that way to save his own skin, but he was going to get a nasty shock.

'My orders are, sir . . . '

'Give me two more seconds, will you?'

The Detective Sergeant and I stood in the wings as we watched this remarkable showman give the performance of his life. Unconcerned he dictated further rapid instructions to his secretary ending with the note that he would be back as soon as possible to take over. So saying, he joined us and walked quietly to the car.

I stood at the entrance of the tent and looked at the two men as they politely begged each other to get in first. It was a disappointingly undramatic ending to a mystery which had been solved in a

221

strange sequence of events. As I watched the car drive off I felt an arm pass through mine and a hand grip me gently.

'You realize, of course, that they've arrested the wrong person?' It was Pascale, warm, young and tender.

'Surprise me.'

'I was with Oscar when the murder was committed. He couldn't have done it.'

'Why didn't you tell the police?'

'They wouldn't have believed me.'

'Why not?'

'Because the real criminal is known to be my biggest rival.'

I froze. Quietly first, then I let the feeling grow on me. It started at the bottom of my spine and moved upwards.

'Could you tell me a little more?'

'Noelle Knowles killed Justin. He wasn't really a very nice man you see. He was ambitious, like Noelle herself. He'd do anything to get to the top. He was a small-time actor when he married Zeelah, through her he met a number of producers — including Oscar.'

As Pascale was warming up to her story Zeelah joined us just outside the tent. A warm wind had sprung up and with the moonlight it was pleasantly peaceful in the quietness of the desert.

'Catching up on the past, Mr. Flute?'

'Miss Anjoux was filling in a few unimportant details.'

'Perhaps I can help.'

So saying Zeelah sat down on a clean patch of sand and Pascale and I followed her example. If the tents had been wigwams we could have called for a peace pipe.

'I was telling Mr. Flute that Justin met Oscar through you.'

'Yes.' It was a sigh. 'One would imagine that it might be difficult to get a part in a film directed by your wife's first husband, but Justin used this odd relationship to get himself into films.'

'How?'

'He worked on Oscar's sensitivity. Told him that hard feelings wouldn't get anyone anywhere and that there couldn't be hard feelings between them if Oscar was big enough to give him a chance.'

'So Oscar did.'

'Yes. After a couple of screen tests

Oscar realized Justin's potentialities — one can't minimize that.'

'How did he meet Noelle?'

'In her first film. They were screen lovers, Oscar saw in them a big publicity stunt and got them to meet off-screen. For Justin it was a marriage of convenience, for Oscar a little painful dig at me.'

From the larger tent a figure appeared. He was a tall man, or so it seemed from where I was sitting, he had broad shoulders and a stance that was uncannily like Justin's. We were in the desert, surrounded by tents, it could be a Roman encampment, it could be Caesar's ghost.

'How ill this taper burns!' I said, looking at the figure.

'I think it is the weakness of mine eyes that shapes this monstrous apparition,' Zeelah filled in for me.

Both women were looking at me with some amusement, it was clear that I had paled a little.

The figure came towards us, the nearer he got the more he looked like Joyce. A thought ran through my mind, a thought about false suicides and publicity stunts, a thought that the man I had believed to be Justin in the studio might have been his double, then the figure got close enough for me to recognize.

'Hi, Joe,' Pascale said.

It was the stunt man, the character I had first seen leaping off the tall building.

'You've met Mr. Adam Flute?'

'I think so.'

I got to my feet and shook the man's hand. He was smaller than Justin and not really like him, but there was this odd resemblance at a distance.

'Joe is taking over Justin's part for the rest of the shooting,' Zeelah said. She seemed to like this kindly, shy, scarred man.

'Long shots all the way, but it means a good credit.'

He wasn't sure what he should do next. Both women were sitting, I was standing, the party had been disrupted.

'I'll . . . I'll leave you . . . promised to play chess with one of the camera boys.'

I watched him go, a slow, calm man who had risked his life enough times not to be too influenced by the crazy film world around him.

'You'd never think he was the cause of it all, would you?' Zeelah was looking over her shoulder as Joe disappeared into the tent.

'The cause of what?'

'Justin's death.'

'What do you mean?'

'Noelle was in love with him. Wanted to marry him, wanted a divorce from Justin.'

'And he wouldn't give it?'

'Can you imagine it!' Pascale chirped in, 'NOELLE KNOWLES DIVORCES JUSTIN JOYCE TO MARRY UNKNOWN STUNT MAN, or STAR PREFERS DOUBLE TO REAL THING.'

'Was that why she killed him?'

'I think so.'

It was difficult for me to judge the truth of this blunt statement. I had only met Noelle twice, on each occasion she had behaved in a peculiar way, dressing up, slightly drunk, getting all confused when she gave me the dope — and then when she had had the argument with Pascale. She had a temper, she was emotional enough and mad enough to do such a thing.

'How did you hear about all this?' I asked. I was still standing and unconsciously walking about quite a bit.

'Oscar told us. He's known all the time.'

I was trying to piece up everything, make a nice square parcel of all the events, but there were still some pieces missing.

'But . . . why did you send me on this wild goose chase after April . . . if you knew . . . '

'I didn't know,' Zeelah butted in, 'I didn't know anything until about half an hour ago. Oscar knew all the time that it was Noelle. He was concerned about the film, so he threw suspicion first on April then on himself in a hope of saving the girl and saving time.'

'But it was a mad thing to do!'

'Oscar is mad.'

'Why did he give up suddenly then?'

Zeelah looked at Pascale who looked back at her and smiled. Zeelah had never been friends with Noelle, but she seemed to like this girl. Somehow Pascale had convinced Oscar that she would be able to take Noelle's part, and that had been the end of Noelle.

'Where is she now?'

'Noelle? She knows the game is up, she knows Oscar isn't protecting her any more. I'd imagine she's back at her hotel probably making that suicide story that misfired come true!'

'She's not on the set?' I asked, appalled.

'No, she left on the back of a telegraph boy's motorbike some time ago.'

14

I wanted to be in at the finale. I had been in at the beginning of this whole affair and I had a Private Detective's pride of wanting to be in at the end. I didn't think for one moment that a girl like Noelle would take her own life, she'd think about it, make a dramatic attempt, but she'd fail to succeed.

I didn't waste any time, leaving Pascale and Zeelah to the torments of the following day's shooting, I got into the jeep that was parked among the lorries, and started it up without difficulty.

It was a two hour drive to Cannes and I was going to try to beat that record. I didn't bother to count the miraculous escapes I had on the way, the misjudging of a few corners, the four walls I scraped as I bounced from one to the other careering down a narrow lane, the old woman I gave a heart attack to, or the young girls I made scream. It was one of those hair-raising rides which one dreams of making when drunk — only I was stone cold sober and scared stiff most of the way.

Outside Noelle's Hotel all was calm serene and stately. No ambulances, no police cars, no cameramen, no crowds. If Noelle had gone into the place she had done so quietly and hadn't aroused anyone's attention.

I wasn't exactly dressed for a walk through the foyer but they were used to film people coming off the set and I certainly looked like one of them. I had acquired the habit of wearing my dark glasses indoors at night so that I couldn't see if anyone didn't recognize me.

The desk clerk told me the number of Miss Knowles's room without asking me why I wanted to know. I took the lift to the fourth floor, walked down the lush red carpeted corridor and hammered on No. 16, as though I was the law itself.

As expected there was no answer. There was no one around either so I bent down and took a peep through the keyhole. It revealed nothing except a wall, or something flat across the room, but it did tell me the light was on. The door wasn't a strong one, it was there for decoration, had been there for decoration for many years and hadn't had a change of locks for years. I listened carefully for sounds, took three steps back, then charged.

It didn't give in to me like matchwood, it gave me the impression that I had fractured my left shoulder, but I had bent something and it was just a matter of perseverence. With still no sounds coming from either in or outside the room, I charged again — using my healthy side. This time I very nearly walked through. The lock snapped off a chunk of wood inside, left a few splinters on the red carpet but otherwise no sign of entry.

Carefully I closed the door and leaned against it to regain my breath and take in the decor. Film sets had been modelled on this type of bedroom suite for years. White and gold Louis XVI panelling, more red carpet, Louis XVI commode, Louis XVI carved and gilt sofa, bowl of modern flowers, Twentieth Century cocktail trolley, 1957 Champagne in 1963 ice, dateless double doors leading to bedroom.

The bedroom was the same only with a double bed instead of the bowl of flowers. The chairs were draped with feminine frippery and a single door led to a bathroom. I knew straight away that someone was having a bath because clouds of steam were rolling out of it and there was the sound of lapping water. If I was going to give her a shock anyway, I might just as well get something for my efforts. She could, of course, be having a bubble bath — I had known other people to indulge in that sort of thing.

She didn't hear me at all, partly because I didn't make any noise and partly because she was busy. The bath wasn't full of bubbles, it was deep blue, however, deep blue with mosaics and shining ornate gilt taps. She was shoulder high in the water and looking at her legs as all film stars do when in their bath. On the floor next to her hand she held a tall glass full of the stuff and balanced on the gilt soap dish was an empty bottle of 'Jolie Madame' a powerful sweet scent which she had obviously completely emptied into her bath from the fumes that reached me and made me giddy.

I was busy examining the shape of her fine back, her carefully shaved neck, her brown arms, sun tanned, her legs which moved like twenty-three-year-olds' legs do. I was taking all this in and enjoying it when I noticed the cut-throat razor just next to the scent bottle.

It was ugly there with its open blade and brown handle and I wasn't sure whether I should leap in now and take it from her, or wait till she actually picked it up.

I had guessed she would think of a dramatic ending and somewhere, no doubt, she had read that opening a vein in hot water made you feel sleepy — if a little sticky. I waited, breathed in the scented air too long and coughed.

She turned round, as scared as a sleeping telephonist hearing a bell ring, then relaxed on seeing it was me. I was apparently of no importance in her life.

'When's the opening?' I asked, flicking a cigarette lighter at the end of my cigarette.

'The opening of what?'

'Of the arteries honey.'

'Oh!'

It was a laugh, a sort of surprised laugh as though she hadn't thought about it. She glanced coyly at me then sank deep again into the water.

'How did you get *in*?'

'Broke the door.'

'Is anyone else likely to come?'

'Not unless you've invited them.'

'No. I've invited nobody. I was getting lonely as a matter of fact. Could you pass me my towel?'

The towel was the size of a small ballroom carpet, deep blue like the bath and as heavy as a tiger skin with the tiger in it. Before I could hand it to her she was out of the bath immodestly showing me her figure.

'Don't catch cold,' I said with a mild tremor in my voice.

Coolly she swung the towel round so that it fell on her back, making sure it would brush my face on its way there. I was recovering from the movement of avoiding it when I found her right there in front of me. I had one hand in one pocket and the other occupied by a cigarette. I was helpless. Quickly she snuggled right up against me, dried herself on my dusty suit and pressed her champagne smelling mouth against mine. I didn't even put up a fight.

'You're strangely cute,' she said with the sort of a smile young girls have when they've drunk a few glasses, 'I like you but I can't respect you.'

'If this is the way you behave when you've no respect for men, it suits me fine,' I said.

She left me simmering against the bathroom wall and passed on into the bedroom. I let her go to give myself the time to work things out. In there there was a bed, she was as hot as stolen bullion and I was here to see that she didn't do anything stupid because I suspected her of murder.

'Why did you come here, darling?' she asked from the bedroom. 'What did you want to see me for?'

'Have a chat,' I said. I was stubbing my cigarette out against the side of the wash basin and giving myself a look in the mirror. I had caught the sun, and gone a deep sickening ochre with white rims round the eyes where my glasses had been. I put my glasses down and turned on both taps.

'What about?'

'You.'

She was moving about now, either getting into bed, or something. I dipped my head into the cool water and felt around for a towel.

'How about spending a few hours with me tonight darling. I need company. I'm in the mood for it.'

This was it. The big invite. Nymphomaniacs were all the same, no romance, no working up to it, wam bam, straight into bed and . . . I straightened my tie, pulled down my sleeves and combed my hair. Flute was always immaculately dressed before going into battle.

She wasn't on the bed or in it, she wasn't sitting in front of her dressing table, or helping herself to drinks from the cocktail trolley, she was by the door wearing high heeled shoes, a long ample sable coat and nothing else.

'I've never done this before in my life and I want to now. I want to go for a drive by the sea dressed like this, with you.'

'I see,' I said, seeing. She hadn't bothered to do up her coat. 'I haven't got much of a car, sweety, just a jeep.'

'That's all right, honey, I have one waiting. Oscar's Rolls.'

I had heard about Oscar's Rolls, it had made an impression on the newspaper reporters when they were waiting for the big suicide story. It was a convertible, white, beautiful, the sort of car that anticar enthusiasts stopped in the street to look at. It was sacred, no one, but Oscar or his chauffeur, was allowed to drive it, and yet she was going to. The rat I smelt smelt of funeral parlours, she was going to take her last ride and me with her for the hell of it.

'Why not have a bite first, a last supper?' I wasn't being funny, I was trying to find out if I had guessed right.

'I'm not hungry, not for food.'

'If you're hungry for anything else, I'd have it while it's there,' I said. Anything to delay her now; anything to get her out of this mood which I sensed would end tragically for more than one person.

She gave the idea a long thought, became modest suddenly, or cold.

'You're not my type, darling,' she said at last. 'Not for this hour of the night. You're an after breakfast man, a post-swim in the early dawn light sort of man.'

'Maybe you ought to go alone. Have a swim and come back. I'll wait.' It was a coward's way out but I didn't feel like going for any ride.

'I want you to come with me.'

I wouldn't have taken it as an order if she hadn't taken a small pistol out of her pocket. It was chromium plated, probably had an ivory butt, a lady's gun that could kill as easily as any other — and probably had.

'Was that the one you used on Justin?'

'Yes. Now come on or I'll have to go through the sordid act again.'

'You wouldn't like to tell me why you did it?'

'I'll show you how if you don't move. Come on, honey . . . don't get me mad.'

Like a lamb to the slaughter I walked forward. I had a vague plan, the moment I could I'd get her under control, but the moment never came.

We went down in the lift, through the foyer, into the driveway of the hotel without me having the chance to do anything. Maybe it was because I knew she had nothing on underneath that made me hesitate grabbing her, or maybe because I just didn't trust her with that gun. She was the type of girl who would fire it and I might not be the one to be hit. I couldn't risk innocent people's lives.

As we reached the Rolls I saw an opportunity to summon help. The doorman, polite as ever and paid for it, opened the door for her and she got in. I could run, I could scream, but she was watching me and telling me with her eyes that it was pointless trying on anything. But the doorman accompanied me to the other side of the car to open my door. 'Get the police and tell them to follow this car,' I said.

He saluted, made me understand that he had understood and smiled.

Noelle started the huge machine and from the word go I knew that she had driven very little before. We got out of the hotel driveway without killing anyone, drove smoothly along the Boulevard de la Croisette and onto the fast road towards Nice. On the autoroute she speeded up and with the speed got better control of the car.

'Where are we going?'

'Italy.'

Why not? I relaxed, or at least pretended to. Under the seat I found a catch which allowed me to slip my seat back a few inches so that I was slightly behind her. The air was warm, smelling of the sea, the car made no noise at all, it was very nearly enjoyable till we reached the busy Promenade des Anglais at Nice. She slowed down, only just avoided a cyclist and as we passed a T-junction, the idiots sounded their sirens.

There were three of them, two police

vans and a car. If they'd wanted to tell the whole world they were after her they couldn't have done better. Reacting as might be expected, Miss Noelle Knowles promptly put her foot flat down on the accelerator and I closed my eyes.

She lost them quickly, the car was powerful, she had no idea how powerful, so she lost them in a race that no qualified racing driver would have dared attempt. We shot down in the curve round the small harbour, then took off up the hill heading East. First I opened one eye, then the other, then closed both as a narrow tunnel loomed ahead. The road was designed to frighten people like me who rode in open Rolls Royces with crazy film actresses, the sheer cliff face rose to the left, the drop to the shining moonlit sea to the right was too high to calculate.

'This is going to end badly I'm afraid, Mr. Flute,' she said, somehow managing to get round a very dicy corner.

'I'm afraid so.'

'As soon as I can I'll drop you off.'

'Thank you,' I said. I meant it, but also knew that before she could safely stop I had a thousand-to-one chance of getting out alive.

'Why did you do it?' I asked — duty to the end.

'I don't know . . . it just happened. I met him by accident in a corridor outside the studio and he started shouting at me. He was livid because I'd allowed Lovaks to put out all those stories about me.'

'The suicide business and your affair, you mean?'

'Yes.'

I wasn't sure but I had the impression that three cars had collided behind us. It was possible that she had hit an oncoming car, just a gentle touch, bumper against wing, at ninety-seven miles an hour.

'He said I was a stupid ambitious bitch and that he knew perfectly well what was really going on.'

'Which was?'

'Me and Oscar. That *was* going on, but he didn't know about the other.'

'Joe the stunt man?'

'Yeah. When I told him about that and my intention of getting a divorce to marry

Joe, he just blew up. He stormed into one of the empty studios, delivered me one of his pompous lectures and ended up by saying that if I even thought of carrying out my threats he'd see to it personally that I was chucked out of the film. So I shot him.'

'Just like that?'

'Just like that.'

We were winding our way down to Villefranche now and she was getting pretty tense.

'How is it you had a gun on you?'

'Oscar had given it to me a week before. For the suicide set-up.'

'What did you do after you'd killed him?'

'Panicked. I didn't know he was dead, I just ran out of the studio, hung around for what seemed like hours wondering what to do, then found Oscar and told him what had happened. He took over from there.'

'Planted the prop sword you mean?'

'Everything. He did everything. It was so easy he knew everyone and knew his way around.'

'It was he who rang me up and told me to go to the scene of the crime then?'

'Yes. I wouldn't have had the imagination to do that.'

'But how did he know I was in the studio?'

'He saw you. He saw you go to the receptionist. He checked up on you, you gave a wrong name or something didn't you?'

'Yes.'

'You were playing right into his hands. Man with false name. Private Dick with false name. A gift!'

Quite suddenly she braked. We were at the bottom of the hill in Villefranche and before us lay the small bay.

'Get out! GET OUT! And if you see him tell Oscar that he should be proud of this, my last performance.'

I didn't wait. I must have had my hand on the door handle because I was in the street before she had said it twice. As I slammed the door and she roared off she gave me a sideways glance and I saw that her eyes were brimming full of tears. It was a desperate moment which I wasn't at all ready for.

Hearing the sirens screaming behind me I leapt to the safety of the pavement as the fastest of the cars tore past. I stood, among surprised sightseers and watched the progress of the mad film star as she drove the Rolls round the bay. She knew the road, she knew the harbour and she had no doubt planned it all in some wild alcoholic dream.

At the best spot she could have chosen she turned the wheel seawards, the car with blazing headlights leapt into the air and plunged some eighty feet to the rocks below.

Monte Carlo had never tried to compete with such a display of fireworks — it was beautiful in all its hideous implication.

The crowds moved forward, ambulances arrived, fire engines, the whole circus, and I watched with a number of others as though I had had nothing to do with it till one bystander, who had seen me get out of the car and realized that I was a potential news-scoop, grabbed hold of me with two of his chums and marched me to the police.

'Cet homme! Il était avec elle.'

'Elle' was now being dragged out of the sea, her sable coat dripping, her dark skin shining in the flickering of the flames and headlamps.

The police were careful with me, word had gone round that this whole case was fraught with strange important people and they didn't dare risk a reprimand. Gently they led me to one of the vans and there asked me to wait till Furrows arrived.

Furrows arrived eventually followed shortly by Oscar in one of the film cars. He had with him five photographers, his secretary and Pascale.

'What did she want to go and use my car for the nut?' He was displeased but dodged around the crowd and the cars and the ambulances then he shouted: 'A shot of her lying naked on the quay — the French papers will use it, get one of her wrapped in her sable for the British and American press. Did she say anything to you Mac?' he asked me, suddenly noticing my presence in the crowd.

'I think she was fond enough of you to make her end dramatic,' I said.

'Yeah? Don't you believe it. That girl didn't do this for my sake, she was nuts. She had some crazy idea that there's a special section in heaven reserved for famous stars, this was her passport.'

I glanced at Pascale who was hugging a linen coat about her.

'Not much sympathy, your boss.'

'He was very fond of her.'

'One would never believe it.'

'Not Noelle . . . his car.'

We smiled. Two innocents in a lousy world of make-believe. I put my arm around her and looked into her eyes to see what there was there.

'You look tired,' she said.

'It's been quite a day.'

'Why don't you come back with me, I'll look after you.'

I didn't answer but let myself be led towards a sports car that seemed to be waiting for her. Looking up I noticed Zeelah and April together in the back of an open Pontiac, two men were with them also, both young, both looking like film stars in embryo.

'Where are you going, Pascale?' The bawl came from Oscar who was directing all the publicity boys in an epic.

'Home!'

'You're missing a big opportunity here — this is the best publicity you'll get for a long time. The scene of the accident will get world coverage!'

'What about Mr. Flute then? He was the last man to be with her, the one she didn't want to kill, don't you think he'll get world coverage.'

The flashbulbs flashed in our faces. Oscar's jaw sagged and I must have looked pretty surprised myself. Neither of us had thought of this but it was too late to back out or have regrets. I got into the sports car, was told to drive off and from Villefranche to Pascale's place in Cannes we were filmed from a van that followed us all the way.

I had one deep regret. I wasn't sure I looked quite famous enough, I had left my dark glasses in Noelle's bathroom.

We do hope that you have enjoyed reading this large print book.

Did you know that all of our titles are available for purchase?

We publish a wide range of high quality large print books including:
Romances, Mysteries, Classics
General Fiction
Non Fiction and Westerns

Special interest titles available in large print are:
The Little Oxford Dictionary
Music Book, Song Book
Hymn Book, Service Book

Also available from us courtesy of Oxford University Press:
Young Readers' Dictionary
(large print edition)
Young Readers' Thesaurus
(large print edition)

For further information or a free brochure, please contact us at:
Ulverscroft Large Print Books Ltd.,
The Green, Bradgate Road, Anstey,
Leicester, LE7 7FU, England.
Tel: (00 44) 0116 236 4325
Fax: (00 44) 0116 234 0205

Other titles in the
Linford Mystery Library:

DEATH CALLED AT NIGHT

R. A. Bennett

Jimmy Ellis believes his parents have died in a car crash when as a young boy he is taken to live with relatives in Australia. The years pass happily, then the nightmare comes. Terrifying images flit through his mind in the dark — all through the eyes of a child, a witness to grisly events seventeen years before. He begins to delve into the past, and soon he finds himself on the trail of a double murderer — a murderer who is prepared to kill again.